VICTORIAN ARTISTS of Wallingford

A Tale of Two Dynasties: **The Hayllar & Leslie Families**

by

Anthony Wilder

Published for the author by
Pie Powder Press

2006

Front cover:
Top row left to right: *'Christmas Eve' by Mary Hayllar; 'The Jester and the Milkmaid' by Peter Leslie*
Bottom row left to right: *Detail from 'The Author's Punt' by George Leslie; 'Study of a Rose' by Jessica Hayllar; 'Lunch Time' by James Hayllar*
Back cover:
'Portrait of Queen Victoria' by James Hayllar & George Leslie

Designed & typeset by Judy & Stuart Dewey at Pie Powder Press
in Zapf Calligraphic & Tahoma using Lotus WordPro
Printed and bound in the UK by Parchment (Oxford) Ltd

Published by:
Pie Powder Press, 16 Lapwing Lane, Cholsey, Wallingford,
Oxfordshire OX10 9QR
Tel (01491) 651127 • e-mail: info@piepowder.co.uk • website: www.piepowder.co.uk

ISBN 0 948598 16 6

Contents

List of Illustrations

NOTE: Throughout the text of this book
titles of artistic works are given in italics with single quotes, eg *'The Gleaners'*.
titles of books and publications are in italics with no quotes, eg *Riverside Letters*

Fig 1.1 Riverside, home of the Leslie family, viewed from the garden which runs down to the Thames on the east

Fig 1.2: Castle Priory from the east across the Thames. The photo was taken by Henry Taunt c1885 when the Hayllar family were living and painting there

Chapter 1
A TALE OF TWO DYNASTIES

In the closing decades of the nineteenth century, Wallingford, a small market town on the banks of the Thames, was a centre of considerable artistic activity. At the time, the town followed the progress of its artists with interest and pride and their work reached national audiences in London and elsewhere. However, in the years that followed their achievements were largely forgotten and it was not until the closing decades of the twentieth century that Victorian painting again began to receive the attention it deserves. The time has come not only to celebrate the work of these artists individually, but also to consider them as a group. For a number of years they drew their inspiration from their home town, its inhabitants and surroundings, and they helped and encouraged each other there.

Their story is largely a tale of two dynasties, each revolving around its own patriarchal figure [see Family Trees on pages 112-113]. These two central figures were **George Dunlop Leslie RA** (1835-1921) and **James Hayllar RBA** (1829-1920). Their lives followed remarkably similar paths. Neither of them was born in Wallingford but they both came to live there at the height of their artistic careers. While there, they both lived in large houses by the river, made a significant impact on the town and were much liked and respected while producing some of their most significant work. Then having stayed for some twenty-five years, they both left to live out the remainder of their lives elsewhere. Also they were both married, both raised quite large numbers of children and, of course, both had other members of their families who were important painters. In George Leslie's case, he was the middle generation of artists. His father, **Charles Robert Leslie RA** (1794-1859) was a major painter of his generation and Professor of Painting at the Royal Academy. George's brother **Robert Leslie** (1826-1901) was a well-known marine painter living for many years in Southampton and his sister **Mary Leslie** (1833-1907) was a fine watercolourist and illustrator who lived in Wallingford. Finally George's son **Peter Leslie** (1877-1953) was a significant painter who started his career in Wallingford. Turning to the Hayllars, James was the first of his family to become a painter but he had four sons and five daughters, four of the daughters becoming major painters. These were **Jessica Hayllar** (1858-1940), **Edith Hayllar** (1860-1948), **Mary Hayllar** (1863-1950) and **Kate Hayllar** (1864-1956). So we have a group of three Leslies and five Hayllars all working in Wallingford.

To them could be added yet another artistic dynasty: **Claude Rowbotham** (1864-1949) lived in Wallingford for about ten years at the turn of the nineteenth and twentieth centuries and played an important role in the artistic life of the town. His work was well-known nationally but perhaps less so than that of his brother Charles and their father Thomas Charles Leeson Rowbotham, both of whom lived elsewhere.

In 2003, The Wallingford Historical and Archaeological Society asked me to give a talk on Wallingford artists to form part of their AGM. I had known of the existence of Hayllar and Leslie ever since I was a child but knew very little about them and nothing about their families. As my research progressed I could see that this was a fascinating story on which I should focus the talk. I unearthed far more information than could be compressed into an hour's talk and people suggested that I should write it up. This book is the result. In doing this research, I have developed a great enthusiasm and respect for the work of these painters and I hope the book will encourage others to enjoy it as much as I have.

Each of these Wallingford painters will be considered individually before we look at their contribution to the town, artistically and socially, as well as their place on the national stage. The evolving position of women artists in the late nineteenth century will turn out to be an important part of the story. First though, we should consider the artistic background from which James Hayllar and George Leslie emerged. This can conveniently be done by looking at the contribution of George's father Charles Leslie.

Chapter 2

THE ARTISTIC BACKGROUND

Charles Leslie was born in London in 1794, the son of Robert Leslie, an American who had come to England the previous year. In 1799 the family returned to the United States. Initially, Charles was apprenticed to a bookseller, Samuel Bradford, but his artistic talent was spotted and he attended the Pennsylvanian Academy of Fine Arts. Robert Leslie had died in 1804 and Samuel Bradford, who had become something of a father figure for young Charles, was instrumental in raising £100 to send him to Europe.[1] He returned to London in 1811 and studied under Benjamin West, the President of the Royal Academy. This American ex-patriot was a renowned history painter and had surrounded himself with a circle of like-minded artists who had a strong influence on Charles. In 1813 Charles entered the Royal Academy Schools where he continued to build on this experience.

For the first part of his artistic career, Charles focused on history painting while supplementing his income as a portrait painter. *'Lady Jane Grey Prevailed upon to Accept the Crown'* (1827) [Fig 2.1] is typical of his work from this period. A strong play of light and dark carries us through the composition. Lady Jane appears to be almost a saint-like figure as the light shines on her. Will she accept her role, the divine right of kings, with all the awesome responsibilities that accompany it?

Later, Charles turned his great skill at figure composition to the illustration of themes from literature. *'Sancho Panza in the Apartment of the Duchess'* (1844) [Fig 2.2] illustrating a scene from Don Quixote, is typical of the work of this phase. Rich colours and an effortless play of light and dark leads the eye around the composition as the figures tell us the story. Charles often used these subjects as a means of commenting on contemporary well-to-do life. Lord Egremont of Petworth, his main patron, described him as 'the Hogarth of elegant life'. Charles spent a great deal of time at Petworth, where the Earl had surrounded himself with some of the leading painters of the day such as Constable, Turner and Wilkie.[2] Another early patron of Charles Leslie's was James Dunlop, a wealthy American who had retired to Devon.

Charles Leslie continued to explore this kind of subject matter for the rest of his life with two major exceptions. These were *'Queen Victoria Receiving the Sacrament at her Coronation'* (1834-5, in the Royal Collection) and *'Fairlop Fair'* (1841, at Arundel Castle), a depiction of middle class life of the time.

Fig 2.1: Charles Leslie - Lady Jane Grey Prevailed Upon to Accept the Crown (1827). Oil

Fig 2.2: Charles Leslie - Sancho Panza in the Apartment of the Duchess (1844). Oil

Apart from a brief return to the United States to teach drawing at West Point Military Academy in 1833-34, the Royal Academy was the centre of Charles's activities. He exhibited there regularly between 1813 and his death in 1859, having been elected an Associate of the Royal Academy (ARA) in 1821 and a full Royal Academician (RA) in 1826, and he enjoyed the comradeship which membership afforded.[3] He was particularly close to John Constable and they conducted a considerable correspondence. Charles drew on these letters when he published *Memoirs of the Life of John Constable* in 1843, which was perhaps the definitive biography of Constable for the first hundred years after his death. In 1847 Charles was appointed Professor of Painting at the Royal Academy, a post he held until 1852. This led to a second publication *Handbook for Young Painters* based on lectures given during his professorship. Notes for two other books remained unfinished at his death and were edited and completed by Tom Taylor: *Autobigraphical Recollections of Charles Robert Leslie RA* (1860) and *The Life and Times of Joshua Reynolds* (1865).

Charles Leslie had married Harriet Honour Stone (1801-1885) and they had three sons and three daughters. **George Dunlop Leslie** was the youngest of these, his middle name given in memory of his father's patron in Devon.[4] The eldest, Robert Charles Leslie (1826-1901), was well-known as a painter of ships and seascapes but also exhibited portraits and genre[5] at the Royal Academy between 1843 and 1887 although he never became a member. From 1865 he lived in Southampton, close to his chief subject matter about which he also wrote several books. The other brother, Sir Bradford Leslie (1831-1926) was a talented engineer who worked for many years in India. He was named after his father's mentor in the United States. Bradford had served an apprenticeship with Isambard Kingdom Brunel, who is said to have waived his fee in return for a portrait of himself by Charles! Of the three daughters, Harriet, Caroline and Mary, it was **Mary Leslie** (1833-1907) who was the artist, but she seemed to need caring for and lived for some years in Wallingford near her brother. In the previous generation Charles's sister Anne Leslie is described in family papers as 'a mistress of drawing', and she is almost certainly the 'Miss Leslie' who exhibited works at the Royal Academy in 1824 and 1825, as her address is the same as her brother's at that time: St John's Place, Lisson Grove.

Not surprisingly, George Leslie was strongly influenced by the artistic world that was so central to his father. By contrast, **James Hayllar** was born into a family with no artistic traditions and he had to make his own way into the world of art, already so familiar to George. Having achieved some preliminary training in Chichester [see Chapter 6], James went to London. Here their careers converged although James, being a few years older, was in the lead. Both boys attended Cary's Art School in Bloomsbury before proceeding to the Academy Schools. Francis Stephen Cary (1808-1880) was a history painter who is now best remembered as a teacher. In 1842 he had taken over Henry Sass's Academy and many well-known painters started their careers under his tuition, including Millais and Rossetti.[6]

James Hayllar attended the Academy Schools in the late 1840s before leaving for Rome in 1851. George followed him to the Academy Schools in 1855 but never studied abroad. Teaching in the Life School at the Academy was shared between the Royal Academicians, each one dedicating a month to the work. In this way students benefited from the experience of a succession of painters who were known as 'Visitors'. By contrast, the teaching in the Antique School, where students worked from casts of antique sculpture, was in the hands of one man. Known as 'the Keeper', this Academician also had responsibility for the running of the whole establishment, and even stood in for the President in his absence. In addition to this practical teaching, lectures were given on painting, sculpture and architecture by the Professors of the Royal Academy Schools. George Jones RA was Keeper from 1840 to 1850 and Charles Leslie RA was Professor of Painting between 1847 and 1852 so young James Hayllar would have worked under both of them. By the time George Leslie arrived, his father had resigned the professorship through ill health, and Charles Landseer RA was the Keeper, a post he held until 1873. George felt that he learned more from the Visitors and from his fellow students than he did from the Keeper, although he later worked closely with the Keeper's brother, Sir Edwin Landseer RA.[7]

So, although their family backgrounds were quite different and their careers diverged for a time afterwards, James Hayllar and George Leslie followed very similar paths during their student days in London.

Chapter 3
GEORGE DUNLOP LESLIE RA
1835-1921

George Dunlop Leslie was born on 2nd July 1835 at Pineapple Place, Edgware Road, London, in the middle of the night. Apparently, a messenger was immediately despatched to convey the good news to his godfather, John Constable.[1] History does not record what his reaction was!

Fig 3.1: George Dunlop Leslie by James Hayllar (1889).

George was educated at the Mercers' School and studied at least to some degree with his father before attending Francis Cary's art school, and thence to the Royal Academy Schools in 1855. He was already very familiar with the Academy, as he explains in his book *The Inner Life of the Royal Academy* (1914):

> *"I suppose that there are no artists living except myself who were ever present at any varnishing days in the forties, and when I tell anyone that I have seen Turner himself painting on his pictures on several such occasions I am scarcely believed. But in former times, Academicians were allowed to take with them, on varnishing days, an assistant; to wash their brushes for them, to carry their paint boxes… And many of those who had sons would take one of them with them in place of such an assistant. Thus it was that I got, on one or two occasions, admission to the Academy on varnishing days when I was still but a small boy.*
>
> *"I knew a great many of the members very well in those days from having met them often enough at my father's house, and amongst others, Alfred and John Chalon, Stanfield, David Roberts, Edwin and Charles Landseer, Uwins, Collins, Cockerell, Wyon, and Maclise; so that I did not feel entirely amongst strangers…*
>
> *"My father also took me several times to Turner's studio in Queen Anne Street, which I recall as a lofty, dimly lit room, very dusty, with numerous pictures stacked round, faces to the walls, and, in an adjoining anteroom, one upon an*

easel that Turner wished to show to my father; there was also on a shelf a row of fat glass bottles, closed with bungs, with brilliant colours in powder inside them. These most likely contained orange and yellow chrome, orpiment, emerald green, red lead, or other pernicious pigments which the great genius delighted in and recklessly employed…

"The only occasion I remember of Turner's visiting at my father's house was in 1850, the year before he died. My father took a great interest in the election of Sir Charles Eastlake to the Presidency, and he invited several members to his house in order to discuss the subject…" [2]

George's first success as a painter came in 1857 while he was a student of the life school of the Royal Academy. He exhibited a picture called *'Hope'* in the British Institution and it was acquired by Lord Houghton for £10. The same year he had his first two paintings hung at the Royal Academy. He was twenty-two years old. Only two years later his father died and so he continued to build his career alone. He is said to have regretted that he never studied abroad in Paris or Rome as many of his contemporaries did, but launched straight into his career.[3]

Many of George's early paintings appear to have been of literary or historical subjects and clearly show the influence of his father's circle. Examples include *'Matilda (Dante's Purgatorio, c28)'* (1860), *'The Cavalier's Escape'* (1862), *'The War Summons, 1485'* (1863) *'Willow, Willow (Othello)'* (1867). The Royal Academy list of exhibitors usually gives George Leslie's address as Abercorn Place until 1871 when he married and moved to 8 Grove End Road.[4] These are both in St John's Wood, London, where a group of artists flourished known as the 'St John's Wood Clique'. George Leslie was a member of this group along with Philip Calderon, William F Yeames, Henry Stacey Marks, and George A Storey. The Clique met every Saturday to draw a given subject and the work was reviewed by the other members. Their main interest was in history painting but, while this was a strong theme in George's work at this time, it was not his only interest. *'The Gleaners'* (1861) [Fig 3.2] dates from this period and is now in a private collection. It is not obviously historical (the costume is roughly contemporary) but we can still see his father's influence in the counter-change of light and dark – the man, dark against the sky and the lady, light against the tree and so on.

George Leslie was proposed for election to Associateship of the Royal Academy in December 1866, the proposer being Philip Calderon and the seconder Sir John Everett Millais. He was elected ARA in January 1868 and a full Royal Academician in 1876, *'The Lass of Richmond Hill'* (Royal Academy (RA) 1877) [Fig 3.3] being his Diploma Picture.[5] This delightful painting, still in the Academy collection, shows the lass sitting somewhat wistfully with her basket. Perhaps she is wondering what the future will hold. The hill is cleverly indicated by the sloping land beyond her.

Fig 3.3: The Lass of Richmond Hill (1877). Oil

Fig 3.2: The Gleaners (1861). Oil

The brushwork is surprisingly loose and on an umber ground, except on the figure herself which is much more closely worked. Young ladies such as this were to be a recurrent theme in George's work well into the twentieth century. They tell us their stories with a quiet sadness as well as beauty, often in a garden. *'The Convent Garden'* [Fig 3.5] is a prime example of this. Signed but undated, this painting almost certainly belongs to the St John's Wood period and is now in The Walker Art Gallery in Liverpool. In it we see a young lady in historical costume contemplating her future. She may follow the religious life typified by the nun. But in front of her, and hidden from the nun's view, is a lute representing the alluring pleasures of the senses. She considers all this in the context of a walled garden. This device strikes a chord. How often do we retreat to a garden at times of decision, to withdraw from the world before re-entering it with a fresh sense of direction? Ruskin, in an essay of 1865 entitled *Of Queen's Gardens* explores the idea of ladies as being the ultimate gardeners and the guardians of virtue in both home and garden. In this he was enlarging on the biblical idea of the *hortus conclusus* or enclosed garden being symbolic of Mary's purity.[6] All this was very much in sympathy with George Leslie's feelings. He admired feminine beauty and he was extremely knowledgeable about gardening. Indeed, the natural world in general and horticulture in particular were his main interests other than painting.

Fig 3.4: Kept in School (1876). Oil

Increasingly, however George was exploring this theme in a contemporary rather than an historical context. In *'Kept in School'* (1876) [Fig 3.4] now in Tate Britain, we still find the garden but it is beyond the reach of the two contemporary schoolgirls who are longing to escape. The garden is made even more tantalising for them by the fact that the window is open and yet what lies beyond is still out of reach. This painting, in common with a number of others by George Leslie, was reproduced as an engraving and was very popular in middle-class Victorian homes. In this way his art reached a much wider audience and he undoubtedly benefited financially.

Fig 3.5: The Convent Garden (undated). Oil

Fig 3.6: The Skipping Rope (c1885). Oil

George Leslie's interest in contemporary settings was to increase in the following years, after a brief investigation of Pre-Raphaelitism. He had never been the most committed to the ideals of the St John's Wood Clique and, although he remained very close to them socially, he felt the need for more artistic space to allow his own ideas to develop. This, coupled with his love of the countryside, especially the River Thames, led to his move to Wallingford in 1883. It was far enough to be away, but still easy for him to get to London in order to fulfil his commitments to the Royal Academy which he took very seriously.

On his arrival in Wallingford, George Leslie purchased Riverside, a large old house by the Thames [see Fig 1.1 on page 6]. He made a number of alterations to the property, creating a fine home for his growing family.[7] In 1871 he had married Lydia Fenwick and they already had five children when they arrived in Wallingford, namely Alice, David, John, Peter and Stephen. Lydia was born in Wallingford in 1883 and with her the family was complete. The 1891 census shows most of the family present on census day. It lists: George Leslie, head of the household, aged 55, Artist and Painter; Lydia Leslie, wife, aged 46; David, son, Scholar, aged 17; John, son, Scholar, aged 15; Peter, son, Scholar, aged 13 (described as 'a cripple'); and Lydia, daughter, aged 7. All except Lydia were born in Marylebone. The family had three domestic servants: Sarah Marcham, aged 28; Ellen Goodwin, aged 15; and Ellen Higgins (widow) aged 22. The delightful painting entitled *'The Skipping Rope'* [Fig 3.6] features members of the household playing in a walled garden. Some are recognisable and help to date the painting. The baby is probably Lydia who would appear to be about two years old, making the date 1885. Peter, with his crutch, is clearly identifiable in the gateway and would have been seven. Judging from the likeness, baby Lydia is being held by her mother, and the boy sitting on the ground would be either David (eleven) or John (nine) The girl about to jump is probably Alice (twelve) and the servant Sarah Marcham may also appear, as she was 22 at the time. The dog looks very like Ben, who is described and illustrated in *Riverside Letters*,[8] but he was only sixteen months old when the book was published in 1896, so this must be his predecessor! The date of 1885 places the scene in Wallingford rather than St John's Wood but so far it has proved impossible to locate it exactly.

George's work reached its maturity during his time in Wallingford. New themes emerged as well as a consolidation of existing ones. 'Girls and gardens' as he himself put it, continued to feature in the paintings sent up to the Academy. Amongst many examples are *'Barbara'* (RA 1893), *'The Ash Grove'* (RA 1898) and *'In Time of War'* (RA 1900) – a particularly powerful image of a girl weeping, sitting on the steps of a sundial. A cat is looking at a statue and there is an empty summerhouse beyond. In *'The Language of Flowers'* (RA 1885) [Fig 3.7], now in Manchester City Art Gallery, the garden, or at least part of it, has been brought indoors. In this deceptively simple composition, the centre of interest is placed in the bottom left-hand corner and the two girls, counter-changed against each other, make strong diagonals stabilised by the verticals and horizontals of the furniture and the panelling. Equally intriguing is the fact that the girl in black looks remarkably like Jessica Hayllar and the other looks like her sister Edith. They would have been twenty-six and twenty-four years old respectively when this was painted and I think they may well have been the sitters.

Another fine example featuring two girls and flowers is *'Sun and Moon Flowers'* (RA 1889) [Fig 3.8]. The background features the garden at Riverside and the water meadows on the opposite bank of the Thames. George tells us that "the whole was painted direct from nature" and Vivien Knight in his commentary adds

> *"One of the girls was a friend while the other was a favourite model of the artist's called Kitty Lambert. In contrast to the fashionable bustles and lacing of the period, they wear softer more natural garments, in a reflection of the aesthetic taste which is also exemplified in the blue and white oriental vases… and the sunflowers themselves".*[9]

All the Wallingford painters used their neighbours, their families and their domestic staff to sit for them and it is fascinating to find the same faces appearing again and again, helping the painter to tell the story.

In *'This is the Way we Wash our Clothes'* (RA 1887) [see Fig 14.1 on page 96] it is Lydia Leslie, aged three-and-a-half, who has been pressed into service. This painting was sold to Lever Bros for £300 to be used as a soap advertisement.[10] It was a controversial move as some artists felt that commercialism of this kind ought to be beneath their dignity. On the

Fig 3.7: *The Language of Flowers* (1885). Oil

Fig 3.8: *Sun and Moon Flowers* (1889). Oil

contrary, George was quite happy to make his art available in a number of unconventional ways, as we shall see in Chapter 13, and this particular painting will be considered further in Chapter 14.

Often sitters appear in George's work as themselves. Portraiture was an important theme throughout his professional life and a number found their way into the Academy – examples being *'Kate Leslie'* (RA 1868), *'Sir Bradford Leslie KCIE'* (RA 1888) and *'Reginald, son of CRL Fletcher, Esq'* (RA 1896). However, it is nice to represent this strand of George's work with an example from Wallingford. *'Portrait of Mrs Phebe King'* (1898) [Fig 3.9] is a large, powerful pencil drawing and reveals a person of sensitivity and determination. Phebe King was a neighbour of the Leslie's who was widowed at the age of 24, with three children to support. George and his family helped her through this difficult time by asking her to take in their washing. Subsequently things improved for her when she married again and started a second family. The portrait still belongs to her granddaughter. Phebe features in another painting which shows her actually doing the washing, an echo of *'This is the Way we Wash our Clothes'*, but the whereabouts of this painting is not known.[11]

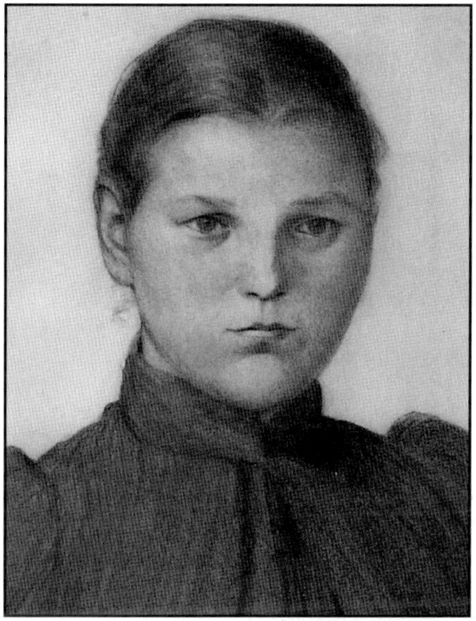

Fig 3.9: Portrait of Mrs Phebe King (1898). Pencil

George's interest in gardening and the natural world was leading him in new directions. In 1881 he published *Our River*, a very successful book about his adventures on the Thames, the people he met, the wildlife he observed and the history of the places he visited. Many of these adventures took place in a punt which George had bought in 1871 and which is featured in *'The Author's Punt'* [Fig 3.10]. This was engraved from a painting and also features George himself with his wife and both daughters. It is one of the many illustrations to be found in *Our River*, which was a great success and ran to four editions. Many of his St John's Wood friends feature in its pages, as does Gertrude Jekyll who shared ideas for his gardening projects at Riverside.[12] This success was followed by *Letters to Marco* (1893) and *Riverside Letters* (1896) which draw on correspondence with his old friend and colleague Henry Stacey Marks RA. In all these books, George shows himself to be a keen observer of the natural world. He delighted in the lives of mammals and birds as well as all aspects of the natural and man-made environment in which they lived. He recorded his observations with sensitivity and humour and his books still make a good read.

Fig 3.10: The Author's Punt (c1881). Engraving. [See front cover for a detail from the original painting]

Fig 3.11: Wallingford Bridge (1890). Oil

Fig 3.12: The Deserted Mill (1906). Oil

In the light of this it is not surprising to find that pure landscape was to become an important theme in his later painting. In *'Wallingford Bridge'* (1890) [Fig 3.11] which belongs to Wallingford Town Council, we find the majestic quality of the trees complementing the architecture of the bridge and contrasting with the delight of the flowers in the meadow in the foreground. The same bridge with its old toll-house appears in *'November Sunshine'* (RA 1895), brightly lit against a dark cloudy sky.

In some ways *'The Deserted Mill'* (RA 1906) [Fig 3.12] could be seen as the culmination of George Leslie's career as it was purchased for the nation by the Chantrey Bequest and is now in Tate Britain. It delights in the colour of sky and water and celebrates beauty tinged with a hint of sadness. This was the last painting that George exhibited at the Academy while living in Wallingford.

After George's brother Robert died in 1901, his widow Eliza Jane and their daughter Kate moved to Lindfield in Sussex and built a house there. Kate had been a frequent visitor at Riverside and now that George and Lydia were approaching their 70s and some of their children had left, it seemed time to move. So George built Compton House on a plot of land in Lindfield which he and Kate had purchased jointly. In 1907 all was ready and George and Lydia left Wallingford for the last time. Mary Leslie moved with them but sadly died soon after their arrival and so the household consisted of George and Lydia, their unmarried children Peter and Lydia and their older widowed daughter Alice Twidell and her son Tommy.[13]

George's painting output slowed somewhat after the move as he was busy planning his new garden. He had also embarked on what was to be his final book, *The Inner Life of the Royal Academy* (1914). This has proved an invaluable source of information about the Academy as George was drawing not only on his own long professional experience but also on childhood memories, as well as anecdotes told to him by his father. It is inevitably written from the perspective of its time and this also makes it very interesting to a modern reader. In spite of these projects, George still managed to exhibit every year at the Academy until his death on 21st February 1921, with *'Bibury, Gloucestershire'* exhibited posthumously that year.

Back in Wallingford, a fulsome obituary appeared in the *Berks and Oxon Advertiser* for 25th February. In it George Leslie is quoted as saying:

> *"My aim in art has always been to paint pictures from the sunny side of English domestic life, and as much as possible to render them cheerful companions of their possessor. The times are so imbued with turmoil and misery, hard work and utilitarianism that innocence, joy and beauty seem to be the most fitting subjects to render such powers as I possess useful to my fellow creatures".*[14]

Fig 4.1: View of Tenby (undated). Watercolour

Fig 4.2: The Last Supper (undated). Pen & ink and watercolour

Fig 4.3: Jesus and His Disciples (undated). Pen & ink and watercolour

Chapter 4
MARY LESLIE
1833-1907

Mary Leslie was born in 1833, the fifth child of Charles and Harriet. Sadly she probably suffered some degree of brain damage at birth and she was also burdened by the loss of sight in one eye. In spite of her difficulties, she was very well-liked in the family, who called her Polly. She accompanied her father on a visit to Paris in 1847 when she was fourteen and in a letter home he writes

> *"Little Polly is regularly admitted a student of the Louvre. How amused you would be to see her sitting in all her uprightness, on a high stool with her sketchbook in her hand and her watercolours beside her, before a most beautiful Terburgh, drawing and rubbing out and not finding it possible to please herself, as usual."*

Tom Taylor, the writer who edited her father's autobiography in 1860, said that Mary had "a rare reach of invention" and he admired her abilities as a colourist and a designer. Clearly the family recognised and encouraged Mary's artistic abilities, but they also saw the need to care for and protect her. She remained with her mother after her father's death and probably went with her when she moved to a cottage on Remenham Hill above Henley in 1869. Harriet's main concern in her Will was to secure Mary's financial well-being after she was no longer there to care for her.[1]

After George had purchased Riverside, he also acquired the next door property, Coburg Cottage, now called Cromwell Lodge. As part of a gardening project, George and one of his sons, built a long curving wall between the two properties, filled with interesting carved stones. He is thought to have used one of the rooms as a studio,[2] but his main aim was probably to provide a home for Mary, as their mother had died in 1885. The 1891 census again makes interesting reading. Head of the household is Robert Betteridge, a retired railway engine driver, aged 62; his wife Susannah Betteridge, aged 61; their daughter Louisa Betteridge, aged 20; Mary Leslie, aged 57, boarder, single, living on own means, 'imbecile'. This probably explains the presence of the final member of the household: Bessie Robertson, boarder, single, aged 37, nurse. Interestingly, Bessie Robertson was also with the household at 8 Grove End Road in the 1881 census but she is listed as a visitor. Her age was given as 22 – she was a hospital nurse and had been born at Tooting.

Fig 4.4: Praise for Mercies Spiritual and Temporal (undated). Pen & ink

To a 21st century reader, this description of Mary's condition seems to be very much a harsh overstatement. A number of her sketchbooks and notebooks have been deposited in the Tate Archive along with an extensive collection of other family papers. One drawing was signed and dated "M.L.1874" but, although most are signed, it is not possible to date those reproduced here.[3]

'Praise for Mercies Spiritual and Temporal' [Fig 4.4] is an exquisite little drawing typical of Mary's fine penmanship. The figures are always very well-drawn and with an assured economy of line, backed up in this case with careful hatching. The subject matter, which is typical of her work, is about social responsibility in a religious context.

In the *'View of Tenby'* [4.1], the pen line is combined with a bright and well handled watercolour. Mary is able to summarise the structure of the landscape while still delighting in details such as the bathing machines all lined up, except one which is on its way down to the surf.

Fig 4.5: Shepherds with their Sheep (undated). Pencil

She showed a similar assurance in her use of pencil, such as in *'Shepherds with their Sheep'* [Fig 4.5], both in the use of tone (left-hand drawing) and line (right-hand drawing). The gradation of tone in the sky and the darkness of the sky against the land, with more dark texturing in the foreground, makes for a convincing and well-balanced composition.

The two illustrations from the life of Jesus on page 24 are probably part of a project for use in a Sunday School. Mary has retold the story in her own words and addressed it to the children. While the figures in the *'Last Supper'* [Fig 4.2] are more naïvely drawn than usual, she is clearly aware of a long tradition of representing this subject in painting. In *'Jesus with his Disciples'* [Fig 4.3], she handles the figures with complete assurance. Each is very well drawn and they are grouped so as to make the meaning clear. Again there is delight and humour in details such as the group of snails in the foreground.

After enjoying work such as this, it is even more difficult to accept the verdict of the 1891 census.

As we saw in the last chapter, Mary moved with her brother and his household to Lindfield, but, sadly, she died in 1907, a few months after their arrival. She was 74 years old.

5.1: The Jester and the Milkmaid (1905). Oil

5.2: Portrait of a Young Lady (1914). Watercolour

5.3: Dressing Up (1914). Watercolour

Chapter 5

PETER LESLIE 1877-1953

Peter Leslie was born in St John's Wood in June 1877. At a very early age he contracted polio. His prospects looked grim, but the family was determined to help him to overcome his difficulties as far as possible. His mother took him to stay in Brighton for some months to receive physiotherapy and the rest of the family kept in close touch. Although he was not able to walk unaided, Peter inherited this determination to make the most of his potential. He was six years old when the family moved to Wallingford. Although as he grew up it was difficult for him to join in all the physical activities of his siblings, he rode around on a pony and went on sketching expeditions on the river with his father. As a result, his artistic talents were recognised. He was trained locally by Claude Rowbotham,[1] then in 1899 and 1900 he studied at the Academy of Sir Hubert von Herkomer RA at Bushey in Hertfordshire.[2] Sir Hubert was a formidable art educator and a well-known painter in his own right. As a result of this experience, Peter exhibited at the Royal Academy for the first time in 1899. He was 22 years old and the work was entitled *'The Orphan.'*

Fig 5.4: Peter Leslie photographed by Norah Pennethorne in the mid 1930s

Peter exhibited every year at the Royal Academy from 1899 to 1919, a total of 43 works. His address in 1899 was given as The Red Lion Hotel, Bushey which was clearly where he was staying during his student days. From 1900 to 1906 he was back at Riverside.[3] *'The Jester and the Milkmaid'* [Fig 5.1], painted in 1905 and exhibited the following year, was one of his last paintings to appear at the Royal Academy during his time at Wallingford. It demonstrates a feeling for tonal contrast and a delight in the play of light through the trees, creating a sense of distance which places the figures convincingly into context. The original has the feeling of a Watteau brought down to earth. The texture of the paint is handled with a confidence which is especially remarkable for one who was to make his name in watercolour. In all this we can see the influence of the artistic background from which he was emerging.

In 1907 and 1908 Peter's address was given as Compton House, Lindfield, but from 1909 to 1917 he worked at 12 Meadow Studios, Bushey, near Watford. He was building his reputation and career as a portrait painter and the vast majority of the works that he exhibited at the Royal Academy during these years were portraits. Those of *'Patience'* and *'Mrs Morgan'* (both RA 1908) were commended at the Academy.[4] *'Portrait of a Young Lady'* (1914) [Fig 5.2] is a fine example of his work from this period. The medium is watercolour heightened with white, especially on the blouse. The identity of the sitter is unknown but we sense a good likeness and her mood has been brilliantly and all too clearly expressed! While not a portrait, the experienced eye of a portrait painter is much in evidence in *'Dressing Up'* (RA 1914) [Fig 5.3]. This convincing composition is a very large watercolour and it is a remarkable achievement to sustain the strength of colour and tone in this medium on so large a scale.

In 1918 Peter returned to Lindfield and the following year saw his final work exhibited at the Academy, *'Janet Anne, Daughter of Col. Whittall'*. It is not clear why he did not exhibit there again but after this time he focused increasingly on landscapes in watercolour.

After his father's death in 1921, Peter lived on at Compton House with his mother and sister Lydia. His younger brother Stephen Leslie (1880-1967) had followed in his Uncle Bradford's footsteps by training as an engineer and working for some time in India. Returning to England, he joined the family at Compton House and together they threw themselves into village life, especially amateur dramatics. In spite of his disability, Peter was very much involved and in 1923 he and Stephen appeared in *Trial by Jury*. They were both basses.[5] Although he had no formal artistic training, Stephen was himself a fine watercolourist. *'River Landscape'* [Fig 5.5] demonstrates a sense of atmosphere and tone and a control of the medium which shows what he could have achieved if his engineering work had left him more time.

Fig 5.5: Stephen Leslie – River Landscape (undated). Watercolour

Fig 5.6: Peter Leslie – Country House (1924). Watercolour

Fig 5.7: High Street, Lindfield (1920s). Watercolour

'High Street, Lindfield' (1920s) [Fig 5.7] and *'A Country House'* (1924) [Fig 5.6] are typical examples of Peter's work from this period. His accuracy of drawing, feeling for detail and a sure sense of the play of light and dark are qualities to be seen in these two examples.

After their mother's death in 1928 and Stephen's marriage the following year, Lydia and Peter moved to Ardingly, Sussex, and set up house together. There Peter continued to earn his living as a watercolourist, travelling around the countryside in a motorised tricycle. Sadly, it was on one of these expeditions in 1953 that he encountered a herd of cows which overturned the vehicle and he did not survive. He was 75 years old.[6]

Chapter 6
JAMES HAYLLAR
1829-1920

James Hayllar was born in Chichester on the 3rd January 1829 and baptised on 13th February in St Pancras Church, Eastgate Square. His father was a farmer, miller, and coal merchant and was well-known in the city. The family were of yeoman stock, originally Quakers and related to Richard Cobden, the famous 19th century advocate of free trade.

Fig 6.1: James Hayllar by Edith Hayllar (1890)

James showed artistic talent and an enthusiasm for the subject at an early age but his father was reluctant to allow him to pursue his interest. Eventually James prevailed and received lessons from the brothers William and John Cantiloe Joy, who were well-known marine painters living nearby.[1] With this grounding he was able to move to London and, as we saw in Chapter 2, he enrolled in Cary's Art School in Bloomsbury in 1842. Francis Cary and his wife were particularly kind to young James and they remained close friends until Cary's death in 1881. James Hayllar's fine portrait drawing of Francis Cary is now in the National Portrait Gallery. With this experience James was able to move on to the Royal Academy Schools in the late 1840s and in 1851 at the age of 22 he had his first work hung in the Academy, a portrait entitled *'Son of R Staples Browne Esq'*. It was either at Cary's School or at the Academy that James met his lifelong friend and fellow artist John Cavell, a relative of the ill-fated Nurse Edith Cavell. Two important events arose from this friendship, both of them in 1851. James became engaged to John's sister Ellen and in October that year he and John set out for two years of study in Italy.

In Rome James spent his time drawing from the antique and making studies from the paintings of the old masters. He and John also met Frederic Leighton there and both are thought to feature in Leighton's first great painting *'Cimabue's Celebrated Madonna Carried Through the Streets of Florence'*. This was purchased by Queen Victoria and is now in the Royal Collection but on loan to the National Gallery. One tradition has it that John Cavell sat for the head of Cimabue.

Their studies in Rome completed, it was time to set out for home. They travelled rough and arrived back in England in October 1853 having walked most of the way from Rome! James was now ready to resume his exhibiting career at the Royal Academy, starting with another portrait in 1854. The sitter was his fiancée, Ellen Cavell, and the title was *'Lady Mynzomdie'* – or 'mine-some-day'! His hopes were not misplaced, as on 8th March 1855 Ellen Cavell and James Hayllar were married.[2] From that year the Academy records usually show their address as 15 Mecklenburgh Square and the family continued to own property there into the twentieth century.[3]

Over the next ten years James exhibited a succession of works at the Royal Academy. Some were portraits but many were history paintings along similar lines to the works that George Leslie produced in his early period. Titles such as *'The Queen's Highway in the Sixteenth Century'* (RA 1864) and *'Queen Elizabeth's Toothache'* (RA 1865) being typical of the period.[4]

However, in 1866 a change of approach was ushered in when James painted *'Miss Lily's Carriage Stops the Way'* [Fig 6.2], which was exhibited at the Academy that year and is now in a private collection. It made his reputation. Children were to be a theme in James' painting in which he delighted and which struck a chord in the Victorian imagination. The poise of the child's stance on the stairs is beautifully observed and the amount of space occupied by the maid's dress makes for an interesting composition. This painting was engraved and enjoyed wide popularity in middle-class homes of the period. The model for the maid was Mary Godsal who worked for a number of well-known artists. She came of a poor family but used her success to educate herself, especially in drawing, after which she 'married well'. Like the painting, this story also appealed to the Victorian imagination.[5] James consolidated this success with *'Miss Lily's Return from the Ball'* (RA 1867), and *'The First Flirtation'*, both of which were engraved.

In response to the reception of these paintings, in May 1867 James was proposed as an Associate of the Royal Academy, his proposer being

Fig 6.2: Miss Lily's Carriage Stops the Way (1866). Oil

Fig 6.3: Plagues of the Garden (1870). Oil

WP Frith and the seconder, Alfred Elmore. Unfortunately, in spite of the support of members in such good standing, the election was never successful.[6] Although he continued to exhibit at the Academy every year, he seems to have maintained some distance from it. Instead he joined the Society of British Artists in 1876 and exhibited with them extensively.[7] This was originally a rival institution to the Academy, founded by a group of painters including John Martin and Thomas Heaphy (its first president) in 1824. In 1887, under the presidency of James McNeill Whistler, it became the Royal Society of British Artists and members were styled RBA. James Hayllar sometimes used these initials. He rose to serve on the Council of the Society in the 1880s and his works were sometimes illustrated in its exhibition catalogues. However, the Council minute book shows that he resigned his membership of the RBA in January 1890. It is not clear why he resigned, but neither he nor his daughters exhibited with the society subsequently.[8]

While childhood was a recurrent theme in James's work, humour was another, often contrasting the image with the title, and *'Plagues of the Garden'* (1870) [Fig 6.3] is a prime example. What a superbly observed child with her knock-knees and the colour of the roses (what remains of them) complementing that of her dress!

Fig 6.4: As the Twig is Bent so the Tree is Inclined (1879)

Another interest was the relationship between young and old. In *'As the Twig is Bent so the Tree is Inclined'* (1879) [Fig 6.4] an old farm labourer is seen teaching his little granddaughter to pray. This expresses the romantic idea that the simple country cottage was the best place to bring up children.[9] The old man's kindly seriousness inspires a sense of wonder in the child, which helps James to express a sort of simple holiness through the painting.

This interest in children may well have been inspired by James and Ellen's own expanding family. Between 1856 and 1868 they had nine children, Ernest Theodore, Reginald James, Jessica Ellen, Edith Parvin, Eugene Grace, Alexandra Mary, Beatrice Kate, Thomas, and Algernon Victor. As the family grew they felt the need to escape into the countryside and in 1865 they rented Carlton Rookery, a country house near Saxmundham in Suffolk, where they spent their summers. Not being a member of the Academy meant that James felt somewhat detached from the art world and his family clearly enjoyed country life. Yet he still needed to be close enough to London to take part in exhibitions, which he was doing with increasing success. As was to be the case with George Leslie a few years later, Wallingford provided the answer. No doubt James was encouraged to make the move because a branch of the Cavell family had been established in the town for some time. James Hayllar purchased Castle Priory in 1875 and George Cavell and James's old teacher Francis Cary appear to have assisted him in some capacity, as they both signed the lease.[10] Castle Priory is a fine old house by the river, once the home of the well-known judge, Sir William Blackstone, and it was to inspire the artistic work of the family for the next 25 years, as well as being the centre for their social and sporting activities [see photograph on page 6]. Apart from his own painting, one of James's most significant achievements was the artistic education of his children. This was particularly true of his daughters, and their stories will be told in more detail later.

The census returns give us a glimpse of the family's artistic activities at Castle Priory. The 1881 census records: James Hayllar, head of the household, aged 52, painter; Ellen Hayllar, his wife, aged 55, born at Grays Inn; Jessica Hayllar, daughter, aged 22, painter of domestic life, born in St Pancras (London); Edith Hayllar, daughter, aged 20, painter, born at St Pancras; Grace Hayllar, daughter, aged 19, no occupation, Mary Hayllar, daughter, aged 18, still-life painter, born in St Pancras. The family had three domestic servants, all of them unmarried: Ann Geaving, aged 26, cook; Emma Nash, aged 31, needlewoman; and Mary Wakeling, aged 23, housemaid. None of the sons was at home on census day and neither was Kate. Ten years later in the 1891 census Ellen is herself described as an artist. Jessica is still described as an artist and Kate, who is known by her other name of Beatrice, is an 'artist – still-life'. Mary is not mentioned as she had married and left home by this date. Edith and all her brothers were also away. The domestic staff had changed but the same occupations are represented: Ann Murcote, widow, aged 41, cook; Mary Tustain, aged 27, needlewoman; and Agnes Perry, aged 22, housemaid.

'The Picture Gallery in the Hall' (RA 1889) [Fig 6.6] is an example of the influence the house was to have on the family's painting. In it we see the young daughter of a manor house showing a very respectful group of villagers the fine collection of paintings that her family owns. In fact the room

Fig 6.5: The Centre of Attraction (1891). Oil

in which James has set this scene is recognisably the interior of Castle Priory with its characteristic low arch. The large painting behind the two central figures is also identifiable, being by TS Cooper RA.[11] The idea of a painting within a painting held a fascination for several members of the Hayllar family. The whole 'gallery' is filled with a warm light that seems to encourage a sense of well being and stability.

In *'The Centre of Attraction'* (RA 1891) [Fig 6.5], now in the Lady Lever Art Gallery, we return to the theme of childhood and the relationship between young and old. The placing of the figures and the play of light over them expertly fulfils the title. The mother is Mary Hayllar, who had married Henry Wells in 1885, and the scene may be taking place in the garden at Castle Priory.

Wallingford is a good place to assess James Hayllar's work as a portrait painter which, as we have seen, was always an important theme for him. He often used a standard format – highly-worked portrait heads, painted in an opaque medium on paper, with very fine brushwork and a totally plain background. A fine set of eight of these are in Wallingford Town Hall, seven by James and one by Edith. They are all of Wallingford worthies,

Fig 6.6: The Picture Gallery in the Hall (1889). Oil

Fig 6.7: Portrait of the Artist's Mother (1873).

Fig 6.8: Portrait of Edward Wells (1886). Oil

two of whom we have already met – in James's portrait of George Leslie [page 13], and in Edith's portrait of her father [page 33]. We will return to this set in a later chapter. However, one of the most telling portraits by James in this format is the *'Portrait of the Artist's Mother'* (1873) [Fig 6.7] which is in a private collection. It reveals a formidable lady, a force to be reckoned with, but not without humour, and we feel that he loved her anyway!

Not all James Hayllar's portraits followed this pattern. Wallingford Town Hall also houses his masterly *'Portrait of Edward Wells'* (1886) [Fig 6.8]. The sitter looks out of the picture not at us but at a point above and beyond us. We are immediately aware that we are in the presence of a man of power and dignity, although not without a touch of kindness. Edward Wells (1821-1910) was a brewer and banker, probably the biggest single employer in the town. He was also a Justice of the Peace, Member of Parliament for the Borough from 1872 to 1880 and four times mayor. He was very active in charitable work, especially in education, and it is fair to say that he was liked as well as respected. This was reflected in his appointment as High Steward for the Borough.[12] In considering the view that James has given us of him, it is interesting to reflect that the year before this was painted, Edward Wells's son Henry had married James Hayllar's daughter, Mary! This portrait also exists as an engraving by Algernon Hayllar and a copy can be seen in Wallingford Museum.

Fig 6.9: From Grim's Dyke (1896). Oil

The Town Council also owns a painting by James that reveals another theme in his work – groups of people in a landscape. *'From Grim's Dyke'* (1896) [Fig 6.9] was originally hung in the Town Hall as a pair with George Leslie's *'Wallingford Bridge'* but they are now both in the town offices. It reveals a group of people enjoying the beauties of a stretch of countryside that would have been well-known to most people from Wallingford, then and now.

Left *Fig 6.10: Landscape with Sheep (1892). Oil*
Above *Fig 6.11: Lunch Time (undated). Oil*

Recent lists attribute this painting to Jessica rather than James, but the local press at the time gave it to James.[13] I suspect that the confusion is due to the two painters sharing the same initials.

Although James Hayllar was best known for the subject-matter that we have already considered, he was also a very fine landscape painter. His work in this area tends to be smaller and he sometimes used watercolour instead of oil. *'Landscape with Sheep'* (1892) [Fig 6.10] which is in a private collection, is a particularly fine example. The landscape rolls away from the spectator whose eye is led along the path, through the group of sheep and into the woodland, where it is free to explore the dark mass of the trees against the sky.

In 1899, this incredibly productive period in James Hayllar's life, centred around Castle Priory, came to an end. As we shall see later, most of his daughters' careers had moved on and the art market was changing focus, so the family's creative momentum was beginning to run down. James retired to Bournemouth and never exhibited again. The 1901 census finds James, retired painter, aged 72, living at Redholme, Cambridge Road, Bournemouth. With him is his wife Ellen, aged 75, and their servants: Jane Cutter, aged 28, cook; and Florence Smith, aged 20, house/parlour-maid.

Shortly after the census was taken, Ellen Hayllar died. Some accounts imply that James lost heart and retired as a result of Ellen's death, but the census information rules this out. Perhaps she was unwell and he became preoccupied caring for her, but this is pure speculation. Jessica moved to Bournemouth with her parents (although she was not at home on census day) and, with Kate's help, she looked after James in his retirement.

'Lunch Time' [Fig 6.11] is a good painting with which to conclude our review of James Hayllar's work, as a label on the back in his handwriting says

> *"'Lunch Time' by James Hayllar. Given to Jessica Ellen Hayllar to be kept as an heirloom being the only drawing left in his possession of this character, 9th Nov. 1912."*

This fine painting, part portrait, part still-life, delights in the play of light over the subjects, which are placed with an unerring sense of composition. The sitter is revealed with James's characteristic sensitivity and sympathy. He was probably the family's gardener and he appears in a number of their paintings, but I have not yet been able to establish his name.

One of James Hayllar's granddaughters, who was interviewed by Christopher Wood in the 1970s, remembered visiting him in Bournemouth. She recalled "a small, courteous and very neat old gentleman with a trim white beard".[14] He died on 10th March 1920 at the age of 92. A brief obituary appeared in the *Berks and Oxon Advertiser* in Wallingford two days later:

> *"... For some years it was our privilege to have him as a neighbour, and he lived at the Castle Priory which he purchased. He was a Justice of the Peace for the County, took much interest in local affairs, and was a sturdy Liberal in politics. He was well-known in the world of art as an artist of renown, and many of his works are owned by local admirers."*

Chapter 7
JESSICA HAYLLAR
1858-1940

Jessica Hayllar was the eldest of James and Ellen's five daughters and was born at St Pancras in London. She was already seventeen when the family moved to Wallingford. James put all his daughters through a rigorous artistic training as soon as they left school. An article in the *Ladies Pictorial* magazine of 1889 gives us some insight into their experiences:

> *"Mr Hayllar superintended his daughters' studies from the days when they were quite children, first insisting that they should learn to draw with accuracy and correctness in black and white. They worked, at first, from the common objects with which they were surrounded. The chief points upon which Mr Hayllar insisted were close observation and great completeness. He made his pupils draw everything that was seen behind and beyond the objects they were studying with the same exactness and truthfulness as the objects themselves.*
>
> *"The Misses Hayllar commenced working in colour after a very few months of training in black and white. Objects were then given to them to reproduce in colour, each object having a special story or interest so that the subjects thus studied formed themselves as it were, into little pictures, which were suitable for exhibition and which readily found purchasers."* [1]

This training took place from ten until four each day. In the evenings there was "modelling in clay, etching or mezzotint engraving on copper". This artistic education was extraordinarily successful in that four of James's five daughters were exhibiting at the Royal Academy at early ages. Mary Hayllar's granddaughter told me that, in response to someone complimenting her grandmother on her painting years after she had given it up, she replied "Anyone can paint if they are taught how to – we were just very well taught." [2]

Grace Hayllar was the only daughter not to pursue an artistic career. However, Anthony Lester reports that she was also involved to an extent as he has seen some very fine drawings by her.[3] She also chose her husband from within the art establishment – she married George Leslie's nephew, Robert Fletcher Leslie (son of his brother Robert) who was a frequent visitor from Southampton.

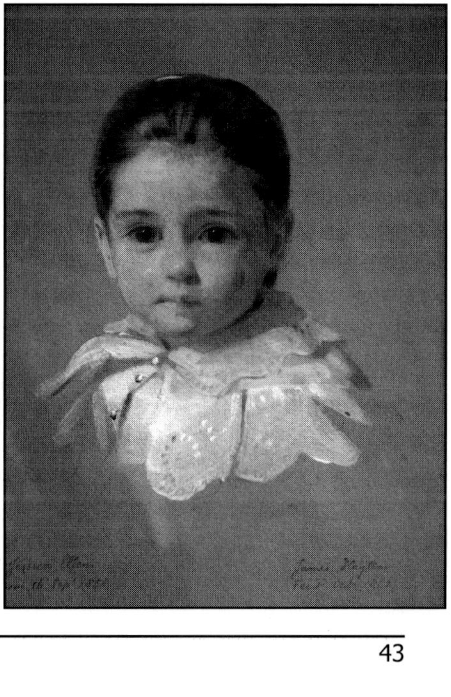

Fig 7.1: Portrait of Jessica Hayllar by James Hayllar (1862)

The sons do not seem to have been put through the same artistic training but one of them did achieve success in the art world, at least for a time. Algernon Hayllar was apprenticed to the engraver Thomas 'Cotton' Webb (1855-1927). Two of his engravings were exhibited at the Royal Academy, both in 1889. One was entitled *'Patty'* and was after George Leslie, and the other was called *'Winley Wind, Durham Coast'* and was after Edwin Ellis.[4] Eventually all four sons emigrated, one to Italy and the others to the far reaches of the British Empire. It is thought, by some members of the family, that this was an attempt to escape their somewhat formidable father![5]

The Royal Academy Schools first admitted women students in 1860 when Laura Hurford got in by default. She presented her work using only her initials and the selectors did not realise she was a woman! They found that there were no rules barring women from entering, so they somewhat reluctantly accepted her. The proportion of women students gradually increased from then onwards, until by the time George Leslie was writing his account of the Academy in 1914, they were in the majority.[6] There was therefore nothing to prevent Jessica and her sisters attending the Academy Schools in the 1870s. Alternatively, the Slade School of Art, founded in 1871, was thought to be more welcoming to women students. It is interesting to speculate over the reasons why James preferred to educate his daughters himself and we will do so in a later chapter.

As a result of her training, Jessica exhibited for the first time in 1879. The painting was hung at the Royal Society of British Artists and it was entitled *'Enough is as Good as a Feast'*. The following year *'Going to my Uncle's'* became her first work to be accepted at the Royal Academy and it was "hung upon the line", ie among those paintings that were most highly thought of. She was 22 years old. Between 1880 and 1915 she exhibited 41 paintings at the Academy and at least sixteen at the Royal Society of British Artists. She also exhibited at Manchester City Art Gallery; Walker Art Gallery, Liverpool; The Royal Society of Arts, Birmingham, and a number of other venues in London.[7]

'A Coming Event' (RA 1886) [Fig 7.2] is a prime example of her work from this period. The subject of a wedding was a popular one in painting at this time, but Jessica has handled it in a very original way. At first sight the

story of the wedding is told by means of a still-life group and flowers that dominate the foreground of the composition. The light shimmering on the folds of the wedding dress is a particularly ravishing passage of brushwork. Jessica also delights in the handling of the flowers which are a recurrent theme throughout her work. The objects assembled in this group, the dress, the flowers, the shoes and the fan all play their part in the ritual of a 'white wedding'. They are all symbolic of the transition in a woman's journey through life that the wedding represents. On closer inspection, the setting (which is, in fact, the inside of Castle Priory) also tells of this journey. The room we are in opens into another in which can be seen the married couple, as it were, a few years hence, and two rooms further on we can just glimpse the lonely figure of a widow in black. We are reminded that the lovely flowers in the foreground will not last forever. This painting helped to establish Jessica's reputation. For many years it formed part of the Forbes collection and was sold at Christie's in 2003.

Rather as her father had done with the Miss Lily series, Jessica followed up the success of *'A Coming Event'* with *'Fresh from the Font'* (RA 1887), *'The Return from Confirmation'* (RA 1888) and finally *'Fresh from the Altar'* (RA 1890) [Fig 7.5] all of which mark stages in a girl's journey through life. In *'Fresh from the Altar'* the story is told largely by means of the people themselves, but there is still room for the flowers and the wedding presents on the table to reinforce the symbolism. The wedding reception is that of Mary Hayllar and Henry Wells, which had taken place in 1885. The tall gentleman coming through the archway looks very like George Leslie and again, Castle Priory forms the setting. One of the pictures on the wall features Queen Victoria's coronation, which serves to link this Christian family celebration to one on a national scale. It is entitled *'Queen Victoria Receiving the Sacrament at her Coronation, Westminster Abbey, June 28th 1838'* and is by CR Leslie. This is probably the engraving by Samuel Cousins. The people in *'Fresh from the Altar'* are very formal, as one might expect, but it seems to me that we are somewhat detached from them. It is almost as if Jessica is observing events from a certain emotional distance. Perhaps it is significant that she herself never married.

Fig 7.2: A Coming Event (1886). Oil

Above *Fig 7.3: The Lemonade Drink (undated). Oil*

Fig 7.4: Study of a Rose (1901). Oil

Fig 7.5: Fresh from the Altar (1890). Oil

In *'The Lemonade Drink'* [Fig 7.3], which belongs to Wallingford Town Council, we find Jessica commenting on a more intimate aspect of the domestic scene. The young cricketer, tired from his game, is revived by a glass of lemonade from a kindly old lady. This echoes the theme of a rapport between old and young which James Hayllar often celebrated in his work. On the shelf behind them we can see an impressive collection of Huntley and Palmer's biscuit tins.

As we have seen, 1899 marked a crisis in the artistic life of the Hayllar family. In that year her father retired from his profession as a painter and moved to Bournemouth. Also, Edith had recently married and given up exhibiting, while Kate changed her profession to become a nurse. Jessica was the only one of the family to continue to paint and exhibit into the twentieth century. She was not unaffected by these events, however, as she moved with her elderly father to look after him in his retirement. In addition, around 1900, at the age of 42, she suffered an accident. According to family tradition she was struck by a carriage and was confined to a wheelchair for the rest of her life.

In spite of all this, Jessica continued to send work to the Royal Academy without a break. From 1899 until she ceased exhibiting, her address in the Academy lists is given as Red Holme, Cambridge Road, Bournemouth. Her subject matter changed somewhat in that flowers, always an important element in her work, now became the dominant theme. *'Study of a Rose'* (1901) [Fig 7.4] is one of a series of delightful studies from this period, which is still in a private collection.

Also in a private collection is *'Madonna Lilies'* (1905) [Fig 7.6]. Although more modest in scale and somewhat more subdued in colour than the paintings that went to the Academy, it is otherwise typical of Jessica's work from this period. The painting not only delights in the flowers for their own sake, but it makes other connections for us. The idea of the Madonna is also presented in the print of the *'Madonna della Sadia'* by Raphael which hangs above them.

Although flowers play a dominant role in Jessica's later work, portraiture was also important for her. The *'Portrait of Thomas Frederick Wells'* (1908) [Fig 7.7] is in my view one of the finest paintings in the Town Hall in Wallingford. She shows us a kindly, scholarly and somewhat world-weary gentleman for whom we feel she had great sympathy. Thomas Wells (1837-1907) was the younger brother of Edward Wells whose portrait we discussed earlier. Thomas was an Alderman of the Borough of Wallingford, served as Mayor four times and took a leading role in the literary life of the town.[8] It is interesting that this portrait was paid for by public subscription in 1908 and Thomas Wells had died the previous year. Either the portrait had been painted earlier or she worked posthumously from photographs.

Jessica Hayllar's career lasted longer than any of her sisters', but she was still only 57 when she exhibited her last painting *'Just Perfection'* at the Royal Academy in 1915. This marked the end of her exhibiting career but she continued to paint at least for a while after this date. The latest painting that I

Fig 7.6: Madonna Lilies (1905). Oil

Fig 7.7: Portrait of Thomas Frederick Wells (1908). Oil

Fig 7.8: Landscape with Trees (1920). Oil

have seen of hers is dated 1920 and is a fine *'Landscape with Trees'* [Fig 7.8]. It is not clear why she did not continue to exhibit after 1915. Perhaps her father needed more care, or perhaps her own health made it difficult for her. When she made her will in 1931 she was living with her sister Edith Mackay at Hill House, Worplesdon in Surrey and she was still there when a codicil was added in 1937. One of Mary Wells's grandchildren told me that she saw Jessica there around 1929 and had the impression that she was still painting, especially flowers, but she had certainly stopped exhibiting.[9] Jessica Hayllar died in 1940 at the age of 82.

Chapter 8
EDITH HAYLLAR
1860-1948

Edith Hayllar was born in St Pancras in London in 1860 and was fifteen years old when the family moved to Wallingford. After her school days were over, she was put through the same artistic training as her sisters. She was ready to exhibit her first painting at the Royal Academy, *'As Hungry as a Hunter'* in 1882. She was 22 years old, the same age as Jessica had been when she made her Academy debut two years earlier. Between 1882 and 1897 Edith exhibited twelve paintings at the Academy as well as at least sixteen at The Royal Society of British Artists. She also sent work to the Liverpool autumn exhibitions at the Walker Art Gallery; Manchester City Art Gallery; The Royal Society of Arts, Birmingham, and other galleries in London.[1]

Fig 8.1: Self-portrait of Edith Hayllar. Oil (undated)

Fig 8.2: A Summer Shower (1883). Oil

'A Summer Shower' (RA 1883) [Fig 8.2] is perhaps one of the most enduring images that Edith created. The whole painting is bathed with light which catches the clothes of the young man pouring the lemonade and casts shadows from the furniture and details such as the tennis balls on the floor, all handled with consummate skill. Edith and Jessica shared this fascination with the play of light, and shared the skill to represent it. Another common theme was the interest in one space opening into another. In *'A Summer Shower'*, once again we are in Castle Priory, looking from one room through

the characteristic low arch into another, and thence to the rain-swept lawn, the river and beyond to the meadows in Crowmarsh. A game of tennis has been interrupted by the weather, and the young players are enjoying a break. Edith was perhaps the most sensitive of all her family at expressing the subtle relationships and rapport between people in her paintings. We seem to know exactly how the young couple in the foreground feel about each other and the conversation they are having, and yet Edith has conveyed this without a hint of caricature. Some writers think that the girl in pink is Edith's sister Grace and the young man would be her future husband Robert Fletcher Leslie.[2] All the members of the Hayllar family were enthusiastic about sport, but Edith reflected this in her paintings much more than the others. *'A Summer Shower'* is a fine example of this – a few moments of relaxation during an enjoyable sporting occasion, captured forever.

Another moment of relaxation after a very different sport is captured in *'The First of October'* (RA 1888) [Fig 8.3]. In this surprisingly small painting, now in a private collection, we see the sportsmen relaxing after a morning's shooting and enjoying a cold luncheon. The simple but effective composition and the play of light and colour serve to hold the many details of the painting together, the dog, the dead birds, the meal and the sportsmen themselves. The pavilion on the right now serves as the bar for Wallingford Rowing Club. It was then in the grounds of Castle Priory, but was never in woodland as we see it here. This is an example of the way all the Hayllars adapted their surroundings the better to 'tell the story' in their paintings. In the same way they would prevail upon their friends, relations and staff to assume the characters which people their paintings.

Many of the paintings under consideration throw light on the way of life and the interests and pre-occupations of middle class English society of the time. Much has been written about the significance of *'Feeding the Swans'* (Walker Art Gallery, Liverpool 1889) [Fig 8.5], now in a private collection. Some say that Edith is reflecting on the woman's role in society as she shows us a young lady helping the little child to feed the swans.[3] Further up the steps we see a young married couple, while at the top of the steps inside the temple are an elderly couple looking on. Their roles and relationships are defined by the steps. Much of this is reflected in the water, and the swans can swim away, but there is no escape for the people.

Fig 8.3: The First of October (1888). Oil

Fig 8.4: Nuts and Wine (1891). Oil

Fig 8.5: Feeding the Swans (1889). Oil

Fig 8.6: Farmhouse Butter and Eggs (1883). Oil

'Farmhouse Butter and Eggs' (Royal Society of British Artists, 1883-4) [Fig 8.6] is reminiscent of Dutch interiors by Vermeer, a school of painting which the Hayllars certainly knew and appreciated. It shares the same stillness and attention to detail as the light plays over the still-life group set in an architectural context. A distant figure looks on. This painting, now in a private collection, is set in yet another part of Castle Priory. It is painted in oil on hardboard, still a relatively new material at the time.

Edith also enjoyed painting still-life in isolation. *'Nuts and Wine'* (RA 1891) [Fig 8.4] is a very difficult subject to photograph effectively. Many telling shapes lurk in the shadows but they tend to be lost in reproduction. The original is a rich and exciting painting.

Edith was best known to the public for the subject matter already considered but she was also a very fine landscape painter. *'Lake Como'* [Fig 8.7] is one of a number painted during a trip to the Alps and Italy, probably in the 1890s. It was painted from the jetty belonging to the hotel where they were staying.

Fig 8.7: Lake Como (c1890s). Oil

As with all the Hayllar artists, portraiture was an important strand and we have already met an example by Edith – the portrait of her father now in Wallingford Town Hall [Fig 6.1 on page 33]. In it, she has deliberately used the same format as he did in order to complete his series of eight Wallingford worthies.

Edith's exhibiting career came to an end in 1897 when *'A Cosy Corner'* became the last painting she sent to the Academy. Shortly after this, she married the Rev Bruce Mackay who was the rector of St Leonard's Church in

Fig 8.8: Eric Mackay as a Young Cricketer (1904). Oil

Wallingford. The 1901 census finds them at the rectory with a son, Eric, aged 1; and a daughter, Jessica, aged 3; together with Anne Chapman, cook, aged 57; and Mabel Hewett, housemaid, aged 15. They subsequently moved to Sutton Courtenay. Edith did do some painting in the early years of their marriage. I have seen a very fine view of Sutton Courtenay Church, which probably dates from this period and '*Eric Mackay as a Young Cricketer*' [Fig 8.8] was painted in 1904. This delightful painting captures their son in a moment of keen enthusiasm. It is a very suitable painting with which to end our survey of Edith Hayllar's work as it echoes her old interest in sporting subjects, while celebrating her new role as a mother. Eric was one of four children born to Edith and Bruce and after this time she appears to have abandoned painting, focusing instead on her work for her husband's parish, and for her children.[4] Eventually, this change was so complete that one of Edith's granddaughters, speaking to Christopher Wood in the 1970s, said that she never knew her grandmother had ever been a painter, until after her death.[5] Edith Mackay died in 1948 at the age of 88.

Fig 9.1: For a Good Boy (1880). Oil

Fig 9.2: Poppies Among the Corn (1883). Oil

Chapter 9
MARY HAYLLAR
1863-1950

Mary Hayllar was twelve years old when the family moved to Wallingford and, like her sisters, she had been born in St Pancras in London. She also trained as a painter under her father and, amazingly, she was only seventeen when her first painting was hung at the Royal Academy in 1880. Entitled *'For a Good Boy'* [Fig 9.1] it features a table set for tea with a view through the window to the river and the Crowmarsh meadows beyond. A lady sits next to the table and a little dog with his back to us begs for a biscuit which is already on the ground in front of him. The warmth of the light in the room echoes the autumnal colours outside. The light falling on the tea-things and the little dog's coat is particularly well handled. This painting was warmly received at the time and more recently it formed part of the Forbes Collection. It was sold at Christie's in 2003 for £22,000. Quite an achievement for a seventeen year old!

This early promise was certainly realised in the quality of Mary's work but sadly her career as a painter was the shortest of all her sisters. She exhibited one painting a year at the Academy between 1880 and 1886.[1] During the same period she exhibited fifteen works at the Royal Society of British Artists, and others at Manchester City Art Gallery and the Walker Gallery at Liverpool.[2]

Children often feature in Mary's work and *'Poppies Among the Corn'* (1883) [Fig 9.2] is a good

Fig 9.3: Mary Hayllar and Henry Wells - their wedding photograph by Latter in 1885

example. In this small painting the brushwork is very reminiscent of George Leslie's in *'The Lass of Richmond Hill'* [Fig 3.3 on page 15]. The figures are finely worked but the landscape is effectively and loosely handled on a buff ground – quite different from her sisters' technique. A label on the back implies that this was exhibited in Newcastle and priced at seven guineas (£7.35p). It was also exhibited at the Royal Society of British Artists where it was worth ten guineas (£10.50p)!

Mary also enjoyed pure landscape, including one which features the Thames just downstream from Castle Priory and on the opposite bank. The carefully balanced composition helps to convey the stillness of the river at this point. A tranquil and contemplative moment.

Like all her sisters, Mary was well able to produce a convincing portrait. Her *'Portrait of John Scott Cavell'* (1884) [Fig 9.4] certainly conveys the determination of the man who had walked back from Italy with her father all those years before. He was, of course, Mary's uncle and a painter himself, exhibiting seven works at the Academy between 1851 and 1862, which he sent in from various addresses in London.[3] One can imagine that he was pleased to sit for his young niece to encourage her. A pencilled note on the back tells us that he was born on 20th December 1820 and died in April 1895 or 1896.

'Christmas Eve' (Manchester City Art Gallery 1885) [Fig 9.5] is a particularly striking work which really conjures the cold of winter. The warm colours of the sunset make the scene appear even colder. We are in the grounds of Castle Priory, part of which can be seen to the left, with the tower of St Mary's Church silhouetted against the sunset.

Fig 9.4: Portrait of John Scott Cavell (1884). Oil

Fig 9.5: Christmas Eve (1885). Oil

Fig 9.6: Helping Gardener (or Gardener's Assistant) (1885)

'Helping Gardener' (RA 1885) is an especially delightful and memorable image, often seen in reproduction today. Also known as *'Gardener's Assistant'*, it features the same man who appears in James Hayllar's *'Lunch Time'* [Fig 6.11 on page 41]. It affords Mary the opportunity to tell a story while delighting in the painting of the children and the flowers and foliage. It also celebrates the rapport between young and old which is often to be found in James's work. In many ways this painting represents the culmination of Mary's career as a painter.

On 1st July 1885 Mary married Henry Wells in St Mary's Church, Wallingford. She exhibited one more painting at the Academy. In 1886 the lists record that Mrs HW (Mary) Wells exhibited a painting called *'On Trust'* and that she lived at Whitecross, Wallingford. It is sobering to note that Mary was 23 years old when her six-year career came to an end, just one year older than most of our other painters were when they started their careers at the Academy. This is at the same time a great achievement and a great loss.

In the years that followed, Henry and Mary Wells raised two sons and four daughters, many of whom feature in their aunts' and grandfather's paintings. Sadly the eldest son, Maurice, was subsequently lost in the First World War. Henry and Mary moved from Whitecross to Sotwell

Hill House in Brightwell-cum-Sotwell, which was close enough to Wallingford for Henry to supervise his family's brewery and banking interests. He also served as Mayor of the Borough in 1902. Mary supported her husband in his work and was also very involved with charitable activities in the town.

The 1901 census finds them both at Sotwell Hill House with five of their six children and Jessica Hayllar who happened to be there that night as a visitor. Interestingly, in supplying the information for the census, Henry makes no mention of her profession as a painter. He also neglects to record her disability but there is some doubt about the exact date of her accident so perhaps it occurred later. Also present that night were: Edith Reeley, aged 27, nursery governess; Emily Hewett, aged 24, cook; Minnie Walters, aged 28, parlour maid; and Maggie Saunders, aged 18, kitchen maid. Ada Polley (later Mrs Ada Lay) was Head Cook in the 1920s and by then the household was served by nine domestic staff, still four in the house, plus three gardeners, an odd-job man and a groom. I talked to Mrs Lay in 2002 (when she was 101) and she painted a vivid picture of life in the household at that time.[4] She thought very highly of Henry and Mary Wells who clearly encouraged a kindly, if disciplined, atmosphere. Although many of the family's paintings adorned the walls, painting itself was strictly a thing of the past. Mary's granddaughter told me that they could not even persuade her to draw for them when they were little.[5] Henry Wells died in a road accident in 1932 and after this Mary returned to live in Wallingford. She herself died in 1950 at the age of 87.

Fig 10.1: Still Life with Strawberries (1884). Oil

Fig 10.2: Sunflowers and Hollyhocks (1889). Oil

Chapter 10

KATE HAYLLAR
1864-1956

Like her sisters, **Kate Hayllar** was born in London, but she was only eleven years old when the family moved to Wallingford. She was soon following in her sisters' footsteps, receiving the same artistic education, and she was ready to start exhibiting her work publicly in 1883 when she was nineteen. The painting was entitled *'Tommy's Orange'* and was exhibited at the Royal Society of British Artists. She made her debut at the Royal Academy in 1885 with *'The Old Brocaded Gown'*. This painting was purchased by the Princess of Wales, later to become Queen Alexandra.[1] Between 1885 and 1898 Kate exhibited a total of twelve works there as well as others at Arthur Tooth and Son's Gallery, the Royal Institute of Painters in Watercolours and the Society of Artists.[2]

'Still Life with Strawberries', 1884 [Fig 10.1], although an early work, already has many of the characteristic hallmarks of Kate's painting. It is tiny, yet with her keen eye for detail, Kate is able to tell us as much in this small space as many other painters would in a painting four or five times the size. It also demonstrates her great sensitivity to colour, never overstated but subtle and profound. I remember the first time I saw this painting, which is in a private collection, standing spellbound by the colour and handling of the shadows on the carved sideboard. Equally telling is the rendering of surface texture such as the glass and the fruit itself.

Kate remained fascinated by still-life throughout her exhibiting career and by the time she painted *'Sunflowers and Hollyhocks'* (RA 1889) [Fig 10.2] her

Fig 10.3: Portrait of Kate Hayllar by her father, James Hayllar (1872)

composition within this genre had become more adventurous. This fine painting, which now belongs to the Corporation of the City of London and is in the Guildhall Museum, reflects an enthusiasm for oriental good taste which was an important strand in artistic thinking at the time.

This theme also finds expression in *'A Thing of Beauty is a Joy Forever'* (RA 1890) [Fig 10.5], the imperial yellow of the walls as well as the upholstery of the chair and the pot on the left being examples. All this is combined with the best that the western tradition had to offer, represented by the engraving of the *'Madonna della Sadia'* by Raphael, which we have already met in a work by Jessica, painted some years later [see Fig 7.6 on page 49]. Kate was clearly very much in sympathy with the aesthetic movement which held that beauty pursued for its own sake constitutes the only appropriate aim of art. The title, a quotation from Keats's *Endymion,* serves to reinforce this view. Seen in reproduction one would be forgiven for thinking that this is an oil painting, but in fact it uses pencil, pen & ink and watercolour, heightened with white and with gum arabic.[3]

As we shall see later, Kate's work was particularly admired at the time but, like Edith, she too gave up painting when their father left Castle Priory for Bournemouth. In Kate's case however, it was not because of marriage but in order to pursue a new career as a nurse. Indeed, a number of people I have spoken to in Wallingford remember Kate Hayllar more as a nurse than as a painter. She never married and seems to have led a somewhat peripatetic existence, staying in the homes of her patients.[4] Before this phase of her career, however, the 1901 census finds her living and working at the Radcliffe Infirmary in Oxford as a hospital nurse. A label on the back of *'Still Life with Strawberries'* says that she made a valuable contribution nursing during the First World War. In this she echoed the work, but not the fate, of her famous cousin, Nurse Edith Cavell.

Fig 10.4: Portrait of Lois Gardiner (1924)

Kate did briefly return to painting, but not to exhibiting, to produce a series of miniature portraits of her great-nephews and nieces. The delightful *'Portrait of Lois Gardiner'* (1924) [Fig 10.5] is one of these. The sitter, now Lois Jenkins, is a granddaughter of Mary Wells. She has clear memories of Great Aunt Kate taking the children swimming in the river and drying them all vigorously afterwards.

Fig 10.5: A Thing of Beauty is a Joy Forever (1890). Mixed media (see text)

Towards the end of her life, Kate Hayllar seems to have divided her time between Torquay in the winter and the Distressed Gentlefolks' Association home at Wallingford Castle in the summer. According to the label on the back of *'Still Life with Strawberries'*, she died at the age of 92, which would make the year 1956. Her miniature portraits, painted in the 1920s and 1930s, represent the last works of these four remarkable sisters.

Fig 11.1: The Thames in Flood (1894). Watercolour

Fig 11.2: The Thames at Wallingford (1902). Watercolour

Chapter 11
CLAUDE ROWBOTHAM
1864-1949

Many people in Wallingford remember the work of **Claude Rowbotham** and although he only lived in the town for a few years, he clearly had a great influence on its artistic life. Consequently, a third dynasty takes its place in the group of Wallingford artists and we should start by placing Claude into this family context.[1]

Claude's grandfather was the first member of the family to be involved in painting. Thomas Leeson Scarse Rowbotham was born in 1783 and spent his early years in Bath. He was a fine landscape watercolour painter, although only a relatively small number of his works are known. This is probably because he earned his living more as a teacher. In about 1812 he moved to Dublin, exhibiting a number of views of the city and its surroundings. In 1825 he left Ireland for Bristol where he played a prominent role in the artistic life of the city along with painters such as William Muller and Henry Willis. Towards the end of his life, Winsor and Newton published a book entitled *The Art of Landscape Painting in Watercolour* written jointly by Thomas and his son Thomas junior. It became a best-seller.

Several of Thomas's children seem to have been involved in painting. Miss E Rowbotham exhibited a number of portraits in watercolour at the Royal Society of British Artists in the 1850s when she was living at the same address as her brother Thomas. AT Rowbotham, who exhibited a watercolour at the same society in 1834, may be another brother.

However, Thomas Charles Leeson Rowbotham, Claude's father, was undoubtedly the most prominent painter of the next generation. Born in Dublin in 1823, he was trained as a painter by his father, but was also a talented musician. He explored a career in this discipline for a while before returning to painting at the age of 22. In the 1840s and 50s he made sketching tours of Wales, Scotland, Ireland, Germany and Normandy. He exhibited four works at the Royal Academy and others at the Royal Society of British Artists and at exhibitions in Bristol and elsewhere but the vast bulk of his output was seen at the Institute of Painters in Watercolour in Pall Mall. He became an associate in 1848 and a full member in 1851 and exhibited a total of 464 works there! He handled watercolour with great assurance and was very sensitive to the play of light over the landscape. He also contributed illustrations to a number of publications on painting and topography.

Thomas never enjoyed the best of health and he died in 1875 at the age of 52. Although he was a fine painter he found it difficult to deal with finance. His fellow artists had to gather round to help his widow, Ellen Amelia, who was left nearly destitute and with eight children to support. In spite of this difficult start, two of these children made their way in the art world – Claude Hamilton Rowbotham, who eventually found his way to Wallingford, and his elder brother, Charles Edmond Rowbotham.

Charles was born in London in 1856 and followed his father as a watercolour landscape painter. His colour tends to be richer than his father's, he made greater use of body colour and was more inclined to include figures in his work. He travelled on sketching tours extensively in the British Isles and also enjoyed the scenery of the Riviera, Switzerland and Italy. He exhibited through a wide range of outlets in London, Birmingham, Manchester, Liverpool and Brighton. As we shall see in Chapter 13, he also contributed to exhibitions in Wallingford, no doubt as a result of his brother's influence. Charles lived at Shepherd's Bush and then Acton in London before moving to Steyning in Sussex and then to Brighton in 1899. In 1913 he was moving again, this time to Addiscombe near Croydon, where he died in 1921. Charles's son Leopold (1889-1977) also has his place in this artistic dynasty as he was trained as a painter but pursued a career as a bank manager.

Now we can turn to Wallingford's member of the dynasty. **Claude Hamilton Rowbotham** was born at Percy Lodge, Campden Hill, London on 6th April 1864. He was only eleven years old when his father died so it is not surprising to find that his early work was very similar to that of his brother Charles. He shared the same rich palette in watercolour, coupled with a use of body colour and an enthusiasm for the landscapes of Italy and the Alps. As his work matured, however, he drew his inspiration from the Thames valley, producing many fine watercolour landscape paintings of subjects from Abingdon to Windsor. This prompted his move to Wallingford in 1893, where he rented a house on part of the Castle estate near Bossom's Wharf. Correspondence with his landlord, John Kirby Hedges, reveals that the property, River View, was fraught with problems. In December 1894, following one of the greatest floods of the River Thames, Claude complained that he…

"… has not been able to inhabit the lower portion of the house since the late flood… all the family feel unwell and even in the upstairs rooms everything is growing mould."

Then in 1895 there was another crisis:

"As my children are now at an age when they begin to notice, the 'scenes' at the Wharf, which have now become of almost daily occurrence, and the language used, are such as to be a source of absolute danger to them and I dare not much longer risk the contamination." [2]

Soon after, the family moved to St Mary's Street at a house called Aureolin. Significantly perhaps, the name is that of a golden yellow watercolour pigment introduced in the 1850s to replace gamboge.

By the time of the 1901 census, Claude had moved to Ipsden, some five miles from Wallingford, but he was still very active in the town at this time. Here we find him living in the school house at Newtown within the village. He is described as a landscape painter working at home on his own account. His wife, Lizzie H Rowbotham is aged 42 (six years older than her husband) and was born at Westerham in Kent. Although they live in the school house, neither of them is a school teacher. They have a son and two daughters: Howard, aged 8, born at Orpington in Kent; Louie, aged 7, born in Wallingford; and Bronwin aged 2, also born in Wallingford. There are no domestic servants listed as supporting this household.

The sense of desolation which the family experienced as a result of the 1894 flood has been brilliantly captured by Claude in *'The Thames in Flood'* [Fig 11.1 on page 68]. The warm colour of the boat, echoed by the distant rooftops, serves to enhance the vast bleak expanse of water between them. This painting has recently returned to Wallingford in a private collection after many years away.

'Wallingford Bridge' [Fig 11.3 overleaf], which is signed but not dated, is another fine example of his work from this period. It shows the bridge on the Crowmarsh side of the river as viewed from Wallingford and features the toll-house which was demolished in 1934. The composition is carefully balanced, with the cows adding interest to the left while the toll-house does the same to the right The washes are very well-handled, giving an emphasis

to the edges of the structure of the bridge and tree trunks. This gives a rhythm which carries our eye across this small but delightful painting.

'Gates of Castle Priory' [Fig 11.4], signed and dated 1896, gives Claude the opportunity to enjoy the texture of brick and flint and to include a characteristic figure to give scale. The crisp morning light emphasises the shadows and verticals of the buildings, the gate posts and the figure, but there is nothing to tell us if she was a member of the Hayllar household who lived beyond the gates!

'Chalmore Ferry' [Fig 11.5] is a larger scale work and a particularly fine example of Claude's painting from this period. Signed and dated 1894, it features a stretch of the river just downstream from Wallingford. The handling is softer than in the previous two paintings and the colour and tones are very evocative of the Thames Valley light which he loved so much and which dominated his work during these years. It affords him the opportunity of enjoying the brushwork necessary for foliage and reflections.

Fig 11.3: Wallingford Bridge (undated). Watercolour

Fig 11.4: Gates of Castle Priory (1896). Watercolour

Fig 11.5: Chalmore Ferry (1894). Watercolour

'Thames at Wallingford' [Fig 11.2 on page 68], a somewhat smaller work signed and dated 1902, features a stretch of the river probably just upstream of Wallingford Bridge. The handling is slightly sharper than the previous example and the composition places the tree on the bank surprisingly close to the middle, but the two share a delight in the reflections and the soft grey sky.

These last four paintings still belong to Wallingford families and Claude certainly had a strong client base while he was in the town. He also contributed greatly to the town's artistic life by his teaching, as we shall see in Chapter 13.

Claude Rowbotham's work found its way into public attention through outlets much further afield than Wallingford. He contributed to shows at the Dudley Gallery in London, Oxford Art Society, Bath and Country Art Club, and Berkshire Art Society of which he was a member and George Leslie was chairman. They held their exhibitions at the Corporation Art Galleries in Reading – Claude's titles included *'The Manacles from the Castle Rocks'* and *'A Relic of the Old Coaching Days'* (1898).

Around 1902 Claude moved to Redruth in Cornwall. From here he brought his work to public attention through one-man shows in London. The first of these took place in 1907 at the Dore Gallery, New Bond Street. It was entitled 'Winter Sketches on the Cornish Riviera' and contained 115 works. This was clearly a success and set the pattern for annual one-man shows at the same gallery. The 1908 exhibition was called 'Watercolours of the Thames and Neighbourhood' with 131 pictures. It was followed in 1909 with 'Sketches of River and Coast Scenery' and 1910 with 'Harbour, Coast and River Scenery'. For his 1911 show he moved to Walker's Galleries, New Bond Street, with 'Watercolour Drawings of Summer on the Thames and Winter in Cornwall' which contained 121 works. His work was also reproduced extensively in the form of coloured aquatints, which were well received by the public.

Around 1920, when he was still only in his mid-fifties, Claude Rowbotham seems to have retired from his profession as a landscape painter and he died in 1949 at the age of 85.

Chapter 12
NATIONAL INFLUENCE

Having enjoyed the work of these painters individually, we can now attempt to put them into their artistic and social context. How was their work regarded nationally at the time? How have they been viewed since?

We can begin by considering to what extent the public was aware of their work. Where could it be seen and what sort of prices did the work command? Then, on a deeper level, what did the public enjoy about these paintings, what sort of critical acclaim did they achieve and what, if anything, did the artists themselves say about their intentions?

Some reference has already been made to the galleries that the artists used and this information[1] can best be drawn together in a table:

	George Leslie	**Mary Leslie**	**Peter Leslie**	**James Hayllar**	**Jessica Hayllar**	**Edith Hayllar**	**Mary Hayllar**	**Kate Hayllar**	**Claude Rowb'm**
RA	113		43	62	41	12	6	12	
RBA	2			143	16	16	15	6	
RI			9	5				1	
ROI			2	4	8	6			
Arthur Tooth				4	6	3		1	
Fine Art Society	7		1		1				
Agnew & Son	4								
Grosvenor	3								
New Gallery	1		2						
Dudley Gallery			3	4	9	1			
Dore Gallery									246
Walker's, Bond St									121
B	1			24	7	10			
L	6		4	17	6	4	3	3	
M			1	14	3	2	3	4	
RHA			1	5					
P			3						
G	2								

RA = Royal Academy
RBA = Royal Society of British Artists
RI = Royal Institute of Painters in Watercolours
ROI =Royal Institute of Painters in Oils
B = Royal Society of Arts, Birmingham
L = Walker Art Gallery, Liverpool
M = Manchester Art Gallery
RHA = Royal Hibernian Academy, Dublin
P = Royal Society of Portrait Painters
G = Glasgow Institute of Fine Art

This information needs to be viewed with some caution. The figures are not complete for some venues and certainly the same paintings appeared in more than one gallery. Also, Claude Rowbotham's output included numerous quite slight drawings which makes it difficult to compare him to the others. Having said that, this does give an impression of the access the public had to the work of these painters during their working lives and the range of outlets used by different members of the group. In addition, during the 1860s and 70s, a number of paintings by James Hayllar and George Leslie were engraved and the prints sold extensively, bringing their work to a wider audience and making a considerable contribution to their finances.

Not only were the paintings exhibited but they were also sold at prices, and in sufficient quantities, to enable these painters to make a living. George Leslie kept a partial list of sales and made other interesting observations in a notebook, which is now in the Tate Archive.[2] For example, in 1865 six paintings are mentioned, one sold for five guineas [see conversion table, left], one for £45, three for £50 each and *'The Defence of Latham House'* fetched £200 at the Royal Academy. In 1883, *'Wayside Rest'* sold for £500 and *'The Daughters of Eve'* fetched £1,000. Both paintings were bought at the Academy by Agnew's. However, by 1900, when three paintings are mentioned, prices had fallen back. *'In Time of War'* fetched £250 and two others were bought by Agnew's for £90 each. George reached his maturity as a painter in time to benefit from an upsurge of patronage. In *The Inner Life of the Royal Academy* he himself explains that a number of wealthy patrons took an interest in 'subject paintings' and the general buying public followed suit.[3]

> *"Visitors at the Private Views in those days really looked at the pictures as well as each other. And altogether the artists had a famous time of it during the 'fifties and 'sixties."*

Later, this sort of subject matter lost ground and many painters had to turn to portraiture to earn a living. For himself, George explains

> *"There is still some patronage, though at a very moderate remuneration, for landscape, and accordingly I have occupied my old age with that delightful branch of painting."*

CONVERSION TO DECIMAL CURRENCY

Note: one guinea=£1.1s.0d=21s.0d

Old		New
one guinea	=	£1.05p
20s.0d	=	£1.00p
10s.0d	=	50p
5s.0d	=	25p
2s.6d	=	12½p
2s.0d	=	10p
1s.0d	=	5p
6d	=	2½p
1d	=	½p

Comparable information for James Hayllar can be found in a series of RBA exhibition catalogues.[4] For example, in 1863 he exhibited four paintings, two for £10 each, one for £35 and the other for £63. By 1889, when he exhibited five works, two were sketches worth six guineas each (a standard price) and the others were worth £35, £73.10s.0d and £157.10s.0d each. In some years he entered as many as nine works. The maximum price I have found was £210 in 1878. Of course, these are asking prices and there is no record of how many were bought but he clearly sold enough and at sufficient prices to make a very comfortable living. Although James inherited some money from his father, as did George, both men had to rely on their painting for the bulk of their income. It was sufficient for both to raise large families in large houses each served by three domestic staff. Figures also survive for a sale of Hayllar family work, which took place at Christie's in 1899.[5] This presumably amounts to a closing down sale when James and Jessica were moving to Bournemouth. Prices for etchings and mezzotints by James range from 11s.0d to £1.8s.0d and, interestingly, similar material by Algernon Hayllar ranges from 15s.0d to £1.11s.0d. Drawings by James range from £1.16s.0d to £7.17s.6d. Paintings by James, which account for the bulk of the material, range from one guinea for 'sketches' to a maximum of eighteen guineas, with most fetching around ten guineas. Seven paintings by Edith fetched prices ranging from £5.15s.6d to £19.8s.6d. Also in the sale were four paintings by Jessica, the only one whose career was to continue after this date. They sold for: one at £7.0s.6d, two at £25.4s.0d each and the highest at £37.16s.0d. One cannot help wondering whether the relatively low prices commanded by James's work compared both to what it had fetched in earlier years and to Jessica's prices, may have contributed to his decision to retire.

During the 1880s at the Royal Society of British Artists,[6] for which figures survive, Jessica's prices ranged from four guineas for *'Poaching'* in 1880 to a maximum of £42 for *'Through the Looking-Glass'* in 1882, with most paintings fetching around £15. Edith's prices for the same period were comparable, ranging from eight guineas to £42 for *'Amy's Birthday'* in 1885. Mary's paintings for the same period ranged from four guineas to £21, with most commanding around £12.12s.0d. Kate's prices at the same venue ranged from £5 to £20. These prices were lower than their father's and considerably lower than George Leslie's, both of whom were at the height of their earning power at this time, even though a general reduction in patronage was probably already setting in. One also has to bear in mind that the Hayllar daughters were still very much at the start of their careers and also their paintings tended to be smaller than many of George's and James's. However one is bound to wonder whether they commanded lower prices because they were women. They certainly thought of themselves as professional painters as their census returns show, and not as 'ladies of leisure' who painted a little in their spare time. Like their father, they depended on their painting for their income, although their overheads were much lower than his as they were all still living at home.

Some years later when Peter Leslie was starting his career, his prices were roughly in the same range as those of the Hayllar women. At the Royal Institute of Painters in Watercolour between 1904 and 1914 his prices ranged from fifteen to twenty guineas.[7] Peter was able to earn at least a modest living as a painter throughout his life.

In the early twentieth century, prices for all the other painters in our group remained low as respect for Victorian painting waned. However interest, and prices, began to revive in the 1970s and 80s. The Forbes Collection of Victorian painting contained an example of work by each of our painters with the exception of Mary Leslie and Peter Leslie. Even taking inflation into account, (for example £1 in 1890 would be worth more than £70 today), the much higher prices they fetched when the collection was sold at Christie's in February 2003 contrasts the way these painters are seen now with the view of their contemporaries. They also perhaps reflect an adjustment in the estimation of the work of each individual. The figures[8] were: Mary Hayllar's *'For a Good Boy'* £22,000; James Hayllar's *'The Only Daughter'* £35,000; Kate Hayllar's *'A Thing of Beauty is a Joy for Ever'* £42,000; Jessica Hayllar's *'A Coming Event'* £120,000; George Leslie's *'Five O'Clock'* £135,000; and Edith Hayllar's *'A Summer Shower'* £320,000.

Turning to the critical acclaim that these artists achieved, it is not surprising to find that George Leslie, as a Royal Academician, tended to attract the most prestigious attention. Tom Taylor commented,

> *"The perfect innocence of his charming maidens whether of town or country, high life or humble – be it Clarissa reading her love-letter by the*

setting sun-light in the quaint old garden, or Celia finding her lover's wreath in the summer house... is as unmistakable as their prettiness." [9]

In 1874 the *Illustrated London News* recognised a degree of refinement in his work which enabled him to portray

"the sweet naïveté and innocence of pure maidenhood with rare delicacy."

George himself observed that

"...all my life I have regarded good-looking girls with feelings of gratitude." [10]

Even more valuable was the opinion of John Ruskin. Writing about *'School Revisited'* at the Royal Academy in 1875 he tells us

"I came upon this picture early in my first walk through the rooms, and was so delighted with it that it made me like everything else I saw that morning. It is altogether exquisite in rendering some of the sweet qualities of English girlhood, and, on the whole, the most easy and graceful composition in the rooms." [11]

This was not the first time Ruskin had commented on George's work. In 1859 he confided in his notebook

"Great impetus given to my painting by a very favourable notice of my pictures in the Royal Academy by John Ruskin".[12]

In a more flippant mood, he wrote to George Adolphus Story RA in 1863,

"Ruskin was at the Academy the other day and looked at nothing else but my pictures and praised them tremendously and said I would be a greater man than my father, but why didn't he buy them? Damn him." [13]

Mary Leslie's work was never exposed to the public in the same way as that of our other painters. However, Tom Taylor wrote that she had "a rare reach of invention"[14] and he recognised her qualities as a colourist and a designer. Now, many years after her death, it is good to know that her work is represented in the Tate Gallery Archive.

The Wallingford Times and *The Berks and Oxon Advertiser* kept the people of the town up-to-date with the activities of its artists and their reports are a valuable source of information. In *The Wallingford Times* of 31st March 1888 we read –

> *"SHOW DAY AT MR HAYLLAR'S STUDIO – On Tuesday, Mr Hayllar, with his customary kindness, invited the residents of Wallingford to his studio, to view the pictures which he and his talented family have painted for this year's exhibition at the Royal Academy. Mr Hayllar's principal picture, 'Gone but not Forgotten' is a splendid specimen of Mr. Hayllar's work…."*

which the article goes on to describe. It continues

> *"The picture is a most interesting one and it seemed to rivet the attention of all who were in the studio. Mr Algernon Hayllar's work consists of three mezzotint engravings illustrating characters mentioned in Enoch Arden. Engravings of this sort were more general some years ago and Mr A Hayllar wishes to revive an interest in them. We must congratulate Mr Hayllar on his son's great success in this branch of art. Miss Kate Hayllar has painted a charming little picture entitled 'The Finished Seascape' which gives us a pretty and highly finished picture within a picture. Miss Edith Hayllar's picture is entitled 'The First of October'* [see page 54] *and portrays three sportsmen who have returned from a day's shooting with an abundance of game and are sitting down to an al fresco luncheon. The manner in which every detail is painted is marvellous, and the picture is a most successful one. Miss Jessica Hayllar's picture of last season 'Fresh from the Font' will be well remembered. The young lady has this year produced a companion picture entitled 'Return from Confirmation'. It is a bright, pleasing work and attracted general admiration."*

A similar occasion was reported in *The Berks and Oxon Advertiser* of 20th March 1891

> *"Mr. Hayllar's principal subject was entitled 'The Centre of Attraction'* [see page 38]. *A fond mother has taken her bright little boy for the old family nurse to see, who, with two aged companions are at the rear of a pretty cottage admiring the little pet, who is proudly displayed in his mother's arms for their inspection. The perfect arrangement of the group, and the completeness and minuteness of everything introduced, stamp the picture as*

an unmistakable 'Hayllar' and one, too, of his very best. Four smaller ones also by Mr Hayllar 'The Thames at Mongewell', 'Wittenham Clumps', 'Horsey Mere', and 'Horsey Marshes' are also masterpieces, notably the former."

Contributions by Kate, Jessica and Edith are described in detail and with great enthusiasm. One of 'Miss Edith's' contributions was *'Sister Arts'*:

"...two young ladies are shown; one is engaged in painting and the other with playing the guitar. Both are well-dressed and as beautiful as it is possible for the heart of man, or woman either, to conceive, and there, with the surroundings of the room, the door of which is open, affording a glance at a pretty profusion of flowers and creeping plants in the garden beyond, combine to make a very captivating picture indeed."

In Jessica's painting, *'A Committee of Taste'...*

"...three beautiful young ladies, beautifully attired, are engaged in the selection of some drapery. The material... looks so like reality that it was impossible to believe it was otherwise without touching it – a test we saw several apply."

References to George Leslie's paintings are often quite brief by comparison, *The Berks and Oxon Advertiser's* piece on 28th April 1901 being typical:

"Mr Leslie's exhibit at the Royal Academy this year is 'The Wishing Well', a girl at a woodland well, and a very beautiful and successful picture it is."

On 3rd May 1901, *The Berks and Oxon Advertiser* reported

"We are very glad to state that three of Mr Peter Leslie's works have been hung at the Royal Academy Exhibition. Two of them are watercolours and one is a pencil drawing. The subjects are 'Sybil', 'A Lady of Quality' and 'A Lady'. We congratulate the young artist on the distinction he has attained and the family on the continuance in it of the hereditary genius."

Both papers are always very positive in their support of the artists, describing the work and then commenting favourably on the fine workmanship and qualities such as delicacy and the refined good taste that the paintings express.

Local papers also reprinted items from the national press that their readers might find interesting. On 13th June 1890 *The Wallingford Times* reported that

> *"In an exhaustive notice of the fine arts at this year's Academy, "Public Opinion" contains the following very complimentary notice:- 'One of the best talked about pictures in the present exhibition is Miss Kate Hayllar's 'A Thing of Beauty is a Joy for Ever'* [see page 67]*... As a tour de force it is marvellous; the painting of the furniture, china, flowers, prints on the walls, is achieved with consummate delicacy; it is harmonious in colour, and so remarkable as a piece of workmanship that one is tempted to think it owes its existence to some clever process rather than to manipulative skill. Artifice can scarcely go further than this...' "*

Sometimes these items adopt are more carping tone, as in this piece from *The Birmingham Daily Post* reproduced in *The Wallingford Times* of 3rd April 1885

> *"We stop for a moment to examine a couple of watercolour drawings characteristic of Mr James Hayllar's bright clean colour and deft workmanship, in which the only defect seems to be that the artist lives in a world without shadow, or with shadows that are only couleur de rose, like the glow cast by the Japanese sunshade upon the face of the sleeping child in 'Under the Haycock Fast Asleep'."*

The article goes on to complain that the child could not possibly hold the handle of the sunshade if she was asleep, and the strawberries were thought to be too red! This delightful painting (or possibly another version of it) must have been purchased by my great-uncle, Frank Wilder, as I remember seeing it in his sitting room when I visited him as a child. He died in 1969 and the painting was sold at Sotheby's in 1974. It was the first painting by James Hayllar that I ever saw and I often wonder where it is now. I cannot agree with the writer of *The Birmingham Daily Post* article!

By contrast, an article in *The Bristol Times* of May 1886 is very positive about Mary Hayllar's *'Gardener's Assistant'* [see page 62]:

> *"It is a charming picture, delightful for its truth to nature and its bright freshness of colour. The figures are admirably drawn and painted."*

The artist may avoid the critic's censure but one of the sitters doesn't.

"Miss Hayllar shows much skill in grasping character. With his shrewd face – a little sour of aspect – he is an excellent representative of his class; not conceited enough for a Scotchman perhaps… but just showing a latent expression of an all-sufficient confidence in himself in a quiet way."

Political correctness was still far in the future! The piece concludes

"The picture is a thoroughly well-considered, well finished work, which cannot fail to increase the reputation of the clever young lady who painted it."

Not surprisingly, this piece did not find its way into the local Wallingford press, where the identity of the gardener would have been well-known to the readers! It was preserved in one of a number of scrapbooks which the Hayllars used to record their artistic output. From the 1880s onwards they seem to have photographed most of the paintings they produced and these were kept in the scrapbooks along with relevant newspaper cuttings.

Sensitivity to beauty, delicacy and good taste, together with truth to nature and a great respect for the skill needed to express all this in paint – these were the qualities that seemed to concern the critics most. On the whole, they were not disappointed with the work of our Wallingford artists.

What did the artists themselves say about their work? So far, I have found no record of the Hayllar women or of Peter Leslie saying anything about it. James was almost as reticent, but an article in *Pearson's Magazine* reproduced in *The Berks and Oxon Advertiser* of 8th September 1899 gives us a glimpse into his thinking:

"For the past twenty-five years, Mr Hayllar has lived in one of the most charming houses on the Thames, close to Wallingford Bridge, and during this time he has almost wholly devoted himself to painting pictures of country life – pictures in which, as he says, he has endeavoured to show the sympathy existing between the well-to-do and the labouring classes. The artist has a store of stories to tell of his models, many of whom are derelicts who have to depend upon what the parish allows them for their maintenance."

As we might expect, George Leslie was more willing to record his thoughts, being a writer as well as a painter. In a letter to Peter, dated June 11th 1906, he is advising him over one of his paintings.[15] He tells him to bear in mind that

> *"the picture is intended to be bought by someone. To hang up and give continual pleasure to the eye but not to worry the spectator with what's it all about or even pester him with obscure and subtle meanings of a didactic, historic or mystic sort. It should be suggestive and interesting but above all a fine piece of good work, good drawing, tone and colour – such a work always finds in time plenty of clever Johnnies who discover no end of subtlety in it and all sorts of high teaching and intentions I don't believe the artist ever dream't about – his simple aim being to make it a good piece of work with a beautiful aspect to it."*

His thoughts on his own painting, quoted on page 23, provide perhaps a more polished insight and one intended for public consumption – innocence, joy and beauty being his watchwords.

Chapter 13
LOCAL INFLUENCE

Not surprisingly, our artists had a considerable impact on the town, both artistically and socially. Clearly, the Hayllar family's open studio days had a leavening impact on the artistic life of the town, and these were not the only opportunities to enjoy paintings locally. *The Berks and Oxon Advertiser* of 6th June 1902 reports,

> *"ART GALLERY – Mr. Rowbotham's annual exhibition of pictures is now taking place in his new floating studio at the Landing Stage. It is without doubt the finest collection ever seen in the neighbourhood and includes a magnificent work by Mr G D Leslie RA, and a host of other well-known artists. There are altogether some 150 exhibits and it would be well-nigh impossible to praise too highly the great excellence of the lovely works on view."*

It is not clear whether another article in the same paper on the 13th June 1902 refers to the same show, although the dates would suggest not. It reports,

> *"THE WALLINGFORD ART GALLERY – The sixth annual exhibition of pictures of Thames scenery at the Bridge Boathouse will be open on Monday next. The work that will be on show is fully up to the merit of the previous exhibitions. Lovers of local surroundings will find a number of excellent pictures taken about Wallingford and the neighbourhood, though other parts of the Thames are not neglected."*

The piece goes on to describe some of the exhibits which included works by Mr Lucien Davis RI, Mr C Dixon RI, Mr Sanderson Wells, Mr Hely Smith RBA as well as Mr Peter Leslie and Mr Charles Rowbotham. Of these, only the last two had any obvious connection with Wallingford, but they all exhibited regularly in London. The gallery was clearly bringing art of quality to the town.

It is clear that things were also happening elsewhere in the county. On 4th January 1902 *The Berks and Oxon Advertiser* reported,

> *"ART IN BERKSHIRE – During the past year, Berkshire has not been behind the other counties in art matters. In addition to the Newbury Exhibition which had a successful season, the Berkshire Art Society's show at the Corporation Art Gallery, Reading, was held in the spring and was*

fairly well attended. Twelve pictures were sold, including those disposed of by the Art Union, which amounted to the sum of £45.19s. The Wallingford Art Gallery exhibition in the summer was perhaps the most successful of all Berkshire exhibitions – no less than 78 pictures being sold of a value of about £200, the Art Union alone accounting for £48. Our celebrated townsman, Mr GD Leslie RA, is president of both the latter exhibitions, and it is greatly to his credit that he should interest himself so largely in the encouragement of art locally, while it is a proud thing that the town should have such a man for a resident and an institution such as the art gallery has proved to be."

Praise indeed! The Berkshire Art Society had been founded in 1899 with George Leslie as president and council members including the architect Alfred Waterhouse RA, EJ Gregory RA, W Henry Gore RBA, and JM Macintosh RBA. Claude Rowbotham was a regular contributor to its exhibitions. Its aims were 'to encourage artists and amateurs, and foster a greater interest in art by the public'.[1] In this, it was the predecessor organisation to the Reading Guild of Artists which was founded in 1930.

Back in Wallingford, our group of artists was encouraging the arts in other ways. An advertisement in *The Berks and Oxon Advertiser* for 1st February 1901, tells us that

"Mr. Rowbotham gives lessons in oil and water colour painting.

"Terms: 3 guineas each term per pupil of about 10 2-hour lessons.
Classes: 1½ guineas each pupil per term.

"All lessons will in future be given in the large new floating studio on the river, or in the travelling studio on the land, thus enabling the student to study painting direct from nature in all seasons and in any weather. There is no system of painting that is so rapidly acquired or of such lasting benefit as that of painting direct from nature."

Claude had obviously thought this through very carefully and it is not surprising that he is so well remembered in the town over one hundred years later. His *'Lower Wharf with St Leonard's Church, Wallingford'* [Fig 13.3 on page 89], signed and dated 1896, is a fine study in its own right but it could have served as a useful teaching-aid for his students. He uses a monochrome sepia wash to create a textbook example of light and dark counter-change on the simplified vegetation in the foreground, echoed by the bush on the opposite bank.

The combined results of his teaching and accessibility to quality painting through open studios and exhibitions led to an active interest in painting amongst a number of the townsfolk. Some of them took up painting themselves, notably Kate Latter and May Walter, whose work can still sometimes be seen reproduced on cards today. Others bought paintings and examples of work by all our artists can still be found in private collections in the neighbourhood.

Other examples of our group's work were permanently available to the public, some of them in rather unexpected venues. *'Wallingford Bridge circa 1450'* was a large drop-scene which George Leslie painted to hang on the wall of the Free Library in St Leonard's Square. It represents the late nineteenth century's best guess at what the bridge would have looked like at

Fig 13.1: Wild flower exhibition in Wallingford Free Library, 1914. George Leslie's drop-scene of Wallingford Bridge circa 1450 can be seen behind the flowers

Fig 13.2: George Leslie's signboard for the Row Barge public house. Although the sign is long gone, this is an enlargement from a photograph of the pub

that time, with the old bridge chapel of St Mary Grace and the Castle beyond. The original is long gone and all we have now are two photographs, one taken in the 1920s by which time it seems badly worn, and the other taken in 1914 when it is in much better condition and in use as a splendid and dramatic backdrop to a wild flower exhibition [Fig 13.1 on previous page].

Also lost is the signboard which George Leslie painted for the Row Barge public house, which was just round the corner from his home at Riverside. This caused interest in the press as he was thought to be the only Royal Academician prepared to do this kind of work, others feeling that it was beneath them. *The Berks and Oxon Advertiser* of 27th June 1890 reports that the signboard had just been completed.

Fig 13.3: Lower Wharf and St Leonard's Church, Wallingford (1896) by Claude Rowbotham. Pencil and wash

"…In his latest signboard Mr. Leslie has taken into consideration the fact that the licence of the house dates back prior to the time of Charles I and that, up to within a few years ago, the house belonged to the Corporation as part of their corporate property. The name 'Row Barge' must have come from some old corporation barge that was used on state occasions, for in bygone days, Wallingford was much connected with royalty and the house, being close to the Thames wharf, was probably frequented by the men attached to the barge. Mr Leslie has taken this idea for his subject and his signboard represents an old state barge rowed by six oarsmen; underneath a canopy in the stern are seated the Mayor and Corporation, while the mace-bearer is in the bows, and a large red flag, with a portcullis, the borough arms, flies behind…"

This was not the only pub sign that George painted. The George and Dragon at Wargrave still has the original board that he and his friend John Hodgson painted, one taking each side, when they stayed there some years earlier and which George mentions in *Our River*. Over a hundred years later one of George's grandsons, John Leslie, became well-known for painting pub signs in East Anglia – yet another family tradition!

Next to the Row Barge is St Leonard's church where worshippers can still contemplate a number of angels which George Leslie painted. They peer down at us from the walls of the apse behind

Fig 13.4: One of the four pairs of angels painted by George Leslie in the apse of St Leonard's Church, Wallingford

the altar. George also designed a stone pulpit for the church, which is now shrouded by ivy in the churchyard.

Added to all this, the Town Council (formerly the Borough Council) owns some 27 paintings of which ten are by James Hayllar, two by Jessica, and one each by Edith Hayllar and George Leslie, together with the portrait of Queen Victoria which James Hayllar and George Leslie painted jointly [see Chapter 15]. They are in the company of works by painters such as Sir Thomas Lawrence and, reputedly, Gainsborough. Most of these paintings would have been accessible to visitors to the Town Hall in the late nineteenth century.

This collection contains an important piece of evidence about the social impact that our group of painters had on the town. We have already encountered the set of eight portraits of Wallingford worthies, seven by James and one by Edith Hayllar. Besides James Hayllar and George Leslie, the sitters included John Hedges Marshall, John Kirby Hedges, Thomas Frederick Wells, Henry Hawkins, Alfred George Field and George Herbert Morrell, well-known bankers, lawyers, brewers and business men in the town. James and George are counted amongst them so, clearly, the idea of artists as subversive individuals starving in garrets does not apply! In fact, both James and George were Justices of the Peace and George was a Borough Councillor.

From this prominent position both families of artists played an important role in the social life of the town and some of their activities were recorded in the local press. Home-grown entertainment involving singing and reciting were always popular. Typical was an event which took place in the Free Library and was reported in *The Wallingford Times* of 28th January 1886. The chair was taken by Mr TF Wells who "opened the proceedings with a few well chosen remarks". Mrs Leslie and Mrs Rothwell performed a 'very pleasing duet' and others, including HW Wells, gave excellent recitations. The bulk of the article, however, describes George Leslie's contribution which was listed as a 'sketch':

> *"Mr Leslie humorously introduced this by saying he had intended to make a picture for them on the platform, but fearing it would take too long, he would bring before them a mechanical contrivance, sent down to him by*

Messrs Maskeleyne and Cook. He then brought on the platform what appeared to be an inanimate object, but which was his little daughter, whom he seated before an easel. He asked the audience to call out the names of any well-known character they would like to see sketched. 'The Grand Old Man' [Gladstone] *was the first call, and he was very truthfully depicted, shirt collar and all. A turn was then given to the Conservatives, who were able to see a fairly good portrait of Lord Randolph Churchill, sketched with great promptitude. Both pictures were greeted with considerable applause, and the audience were very grateful to Mr and Miss Leslie for a pleasant variation in the programme."*

The press coverage of our artists' activities as well as George Leslie's writings give us an impression of people who were able to establish a rapport with a wide range of individuals – from famous players in the art world to local people who had come on hard times and, it would seem, every condition in between. The letter here in Fig 13.5, for example, shows George's kindness in giving his autograph to a young admirer.

Fig 13.5: Letter dated 1 August 1868 from George Leslie to an admirer of his work. It reads "My autograph, such as it is, is most heartily at your service - allow me to thank you for the honour you have done me in thinking it worth a place in your collection. Yours very truly, George D Leslie"

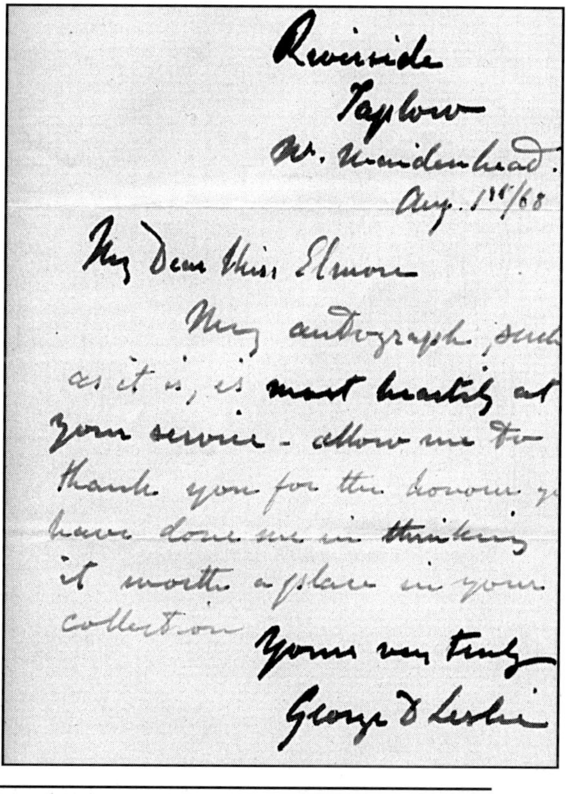
Riverside
Taplow
Nr. Maidenhead.
Aug. 1st/68

My Dear Miss Elmore

My autograph, such as it is, is most heartily at your service - allow me to thank you for the honour you have done me in thinking it worth a place in your collection

Yours very truly
George D Leslie

The Ladies Pictorial Magazine, which gave us details of the Hayllar sisters' artistic education, also mentions their sporting activities:

"The house is beautifully situated on the banks of the Thames, surrounded by lovely elms, and with lawns sloping down to the river so that these most industrious and hardworking lady artists can enjoy such recreation as rowing, punting, tennis and archery after the labours of the day come to an end."

They clearly pursued these activities very seriously as an item in *The Berks and Oxon Advertiser* for 2nd June 1893 records an archery contest between St John's College Oxford and a local team called 'Hill and Valley' which won easily. 'Hill and Valley' consisted of Mr HW Wells, Mr J Hayllar, Mrs HW Wells, Mr R Leslie, Miss E Hayllar and Miss Freely.

The river featured in many of these leisure activities and as well as taking part, some of our painters were involved in organising events. As part of the town's celebrations for Queen

Victoria's Diamond Jubilee in 1897, a water carnival and procession of decorated and illuminated boats took place.[2] The water carnival committee consisted of GD Leslie, James Hayllar, EB Mackay, Richard Wilder and Percy Turner. St Leonard's Church was heavily represented on this committee as E Bruce Mackay was the rector, (shortly to marry Edith Hayllar) while George Leslie and my relative Richard Wilder were his Churchwardens.

George Leslie took his role as Churchwarden very seriously. Several pieces appear in the local papers concerning this activity, perhaps the most notable being *The Wallingford Times* of 28th December 1887. The parish needed a church house for mother's meetings, Sunday school and a proposed working-men's club, as the current arrangements were inadequate.

> *"Mr Leslie having purchased a suitable site, he stated that he was willing to build a church house from the designs of Mr Johns, and would let it to the parish on easy terms with the option of securing the freehold by paying instalments from time to time."*

The vestry meeting accepted his offer.

The same architect worked with George Leslie on what was arguably his most lasting contribution as a Borough Councillor. The Town Hall, which was built in 1670, provides a characteristic and much loved focus to the Market Place. However, by the late 19th century it was thought to be out-of-date and there were moves to demolish it and replace it with a more convenient modern building as a way of celebrating the Queen's Golden Jubilee. George Leslie was in the lead in opposing this, suggesting instead that the existing building should be renovated and updated in a way that was sympathetic to its character. His view prevailed and the work was completed in time for a Grand Corporation Ball to re-open the building as reported by *The Wallingford Times* of 4th November 1887:

> *"Mr Johns, the architect, has carried out his work well, and the thanks of the public are also due to Mr GD Leslie RA, for the manner in which he has devoted so much of his valuable time in his laudable efforts to see that all the characteristic features of the old hall were preserved."*

Chapter 14

DYNASTIES, GROUPS AND WOMEN ARTISTS

The story of art includes a number of examples of groups of artists gathering together for a few years in a particular place. Each artist has an influence on the work of the others and the name of the place often becomes associated with this output. Such groups tend to consist of like-minded individuals, often of roughly the same age, who develop a programme for their art, which then has an influence on artistic developments elsewhere. The Camden Town Group, St Ives, and The Barbizon School all spring to mind. Being a loyal Wallingfordian, when I first embarked on this study I thought how good it would be if it revealed a hitherto unrecognised 'Wallingford Group'! Many of the characteristics that one might look for in such a group are indeed represented in the work of our artists, but others are not.

As we have seen, the work of our painters certainly had significance, and found an audience, well beyond the locality. They also exercised a strong influence on each other, which we will explore further in this chapter. The difference is that in other groups the individuals came together voluntarily, often with a particular artistic programme or project in mind. With our group, only George Leslie and James Hayllar chose to come to Wallingford, later to be joined by Claude Rowbotham. All the others were there because they were dependent on other members of their families; they were brought up there as children or, in Mary Leslie's case, her particular circumstances made her dependent on her brother. Two generations are represented in our group whereas other groups tend to have members of a more consistent age. Those who chose Wallingford were at the height of their careers while the others, except Mary Leslie, were starting theirs. All this means that the influences they brought to bear on each other were structured very differently from those in other, better known, groups. It also means that they did not have a preconceived artistic programme. However, they certainly responded to the artistic and philosophical ideas of the time and each influenced the others in these responses.

Both James and George had reached that stage in their careers where they felt the need for some emotional as well as physical distance between themselves and the art establishment, and yet they both still needed to be part of it. Wallingford provided the answer both in terms of its distance from London and its rural setting. George was able to explore his theme of 'girls and gardens' in congenial surroundings, while James drew inspiration from local people in his exploration of social relations and of childhood. Both painters were well aware of artistic thinking in London and the way it met the needs of the buying public. They saw no conflict between providing patrons with what they wanted and educating and 'improving' them by celebrating beauty. Each in their own way made sure that their children were educated to reflect this in their own emerging work. Later, as the market shifted, both painters turned in varying degrees to landscape and it was at this point that Claude Rowbotham arrived in the town.

Apart from contemporary thinking, painting from earlier periods also had an influence. Both George and James had received a thorough grounding in art history and they passed this understanding on to the next generation. This knowledge is often evident in the form of paintings within paintings, two examples being Jessica and Kate's quotations of Raphael's *Madonna Della Sadia* in their works. Paintings from the 17th century Dutch school clearly exercised a strong fascination, with their calm atmosphere and attention to detail, and this is arguably the strongest single influence from the past.

A more contemporary influence was that of photography. The Hayllar family used photography extensively to record their painting output and its influence may be discernible in some of their compositional devices. Their interest in one interior space opening into another sometimes shows evidence of this, in the same way that it did for Degas. George Leslie specifically recognised the value of photography as an aid in portraiture, as we shall see in the next chapter.

The influence of the aesthetic movement in painting was mentioned in Chapter 10. All our Wallingford painters were concerned with a celebration of beauty in their art. I think their enthusiasm for the aesthetic movement was underpinned by their Christian faith. This is obvious in the case of Mary Leslie whose illustrative work often has a clear Christian message and in some cases was intended for use in a Sunday School. Jessica often refers to Christian celebrations such as confirmation and marriage in her painting. But for all of them, beauty, purity and innocence – whether seen in people and the relations between them, in still-life objects, flowers or landscape – were qualities to be celebrated as evidence of God's handiwork. If the people who bought their paintings were struggling with the darker side of life, wouldn't the contemplation of beauty help in bringing a sense of comfort and peace? Our artists would not have seen this as ignoring evil, or as escapism, but as a modest contribution towards healing it. This concern was expressed by each of our painters in other ways.

George was clearly a devout Christian. He confided in his note book,

> *"I believe the only evil in the next world we have to fear is the remorse for not having done as much as we ought to in this world – and that our greatest blessing there will be for our souls to have a pure and true appreciation of God's love and infinite perfectness to us in this world. God is love."* [1]

As we have seen, he took his work as Churchwarden very seriously and in a practical way. For his part, James had a strong social conscience which was expressed through liberal politics as well as painting.[2] Edith married a clergyman and devoted the rest of her life to helping him care for his parishioners. Mary and Henry Wells started and ended each day with prayers attended by their domestic staff,[3] while Kate cared for people through nursing. In these ways, for the Hayllar daughters at least, this theme outlived their painting and found expression in new activities.

Within our group, the influence of one generation on the next in each family is very clear and we have already seen that the young Peter Leslie was taught by Claude Rowbotham. But how much influence did the Hayllar and Leslie families have on each other? George and James were clearly friends and respected each other's work. In the next chapter we shall see them collaborating but they also shared ideas for artistic projects. We have already considered George Leslie's *'This is the Way we Wash our Clothes'* [see page 19 and Fig 14.1 overleaf]. In *Victorian and Edwardian Paintings in the Lady Lever Art Gallery* Edward Morris refers to it when he writes,

> *"this painting must be closely related to James Hayllar's 'Soap Suds'* [see Fig 14.2 overleaf]. *Leslie and Hayllar were close friends and lived next door to each other in Wallingford… both paintings are very similar in conception and in composition, both were used as soap advertisements - Leslie's painting by Lever for Lever Brothers and 'Soap Suds' by TL Barratt for*

A&F Pears. 'Soap Suds' is now lost and cannot be dated from exhibition catalogues; it is therefore unclear whether Leslie was imitating Hayllar or Hayllar, Leslie in the subject and treatment of the pictures and also uncertain whether Lever was following Barratt or Barratt, Lever in the use of very similar images to advertise soap."[4]

Given George Leslie's enthusiasm for the Royal Academy and James Hayllar's membership of the Royal Society of British Artists, I wondered

Fig 14.1: This is the Way We Wash Our Clothes by George Leslie (1887).

Fig 14.2: Soap Suds by James Hayllar (c1887).

whether this had been a cause of friction between them. The RBA was originally established as a rival institution to the Academy, although by the late 19th century this had eased somewhat. Also, artists with strong views and working in close proximity are renowned for arguing. There is no suggestion of any of this in anything I have read. George and James seemed to treat each other with consistent kindness and respect as brother professionals.

The Hayllar daughters were also familiar with the Leslie household. *The Ladies Pictorial Magazine* article of 1889 which we have quoted before tells us that

> *"Miss Jessica has also found many charming subjects for her brush in the house of her father's next door neighbour, Mr GD Leslie RA."*

Arguably, the influence of George's brushwork can be seen in Mary Hayllar's work. Further evidence of the closeness of the two families is revealed in a scrapbook which one of Edith's daughters, Margaret Mackay kept in the 1900s. Margaret, who was herself a very talented watercolourist, writes in the front "This album is reserved for articles and noteworthy personages only, Peggy Mackay, Sutton Courtenay Vicarage". In it can be found a delightful watercolour of Lake Lucerne dated February 1910 by Edith, the latest work by her that I have seen. On the next page is a study of flowers dated 1914 by Jessica. Also to be found is a drawing by George Leslie dated 1911 and a pen portrait of a soldier entitled *'Hospital Days'* by Peter Leslie, dated 1917. It is significant that these artists were clearly still in touch some years after they had all left Wallingford.

Perhaps these contacts helped to ease the pressures that inevitably exist within dynasties. Choosing to follow the same profession as one's father, especially if that profession is painting, has many challenges as well as advantages. Those concerned grow up steeped in the atmosphere of the subject and gain an instinctive feeling for it, and they know many of the key players of the previous generation. Out of respect for the father, these established painters will probably help the newcomers as they embark on their careers. However, the father may try to exercise undue influence over his offspring's progress. He may try to mould them in his own image or make well-intentioned efforts to help them avoid the mistakes which, with hindsight, he now realises he made. More seriously, the children are embarking on their careers when the father is at the height of his. They may compare themselves to him and feel inadequate. It is all too easy for them to carry a burden of undue self-criticism. Also, other people have an ambivalent view of dynasties. On the one hand they find them fascinating and rather like the idea of a creative family tradition. On the other hand, they constantly compare one member with another. Colleagues may feel that these younger members of dynasties have only achieved through the efforts of the previous generation and that they would not have succeeded if they had had to make their own way in the world, as others do. This may well feed a sense of unease. Many of these tensions are evident in the relations between Charles, George and Peter Leslie and we found them hinted at in Chapter 12 where George was advising Peter on his work [see page 84]. For his part, George confides in his notebook,

> *"great impetus given to my painting… on account of the death of my dear father who died Thursday 5th of May 1859 and consequently placed me on my own resources. May the Almighty give me strength and health to paint something worthy of my name before I die. Amen."*[5]

If these tensions were present for the Leslies, they were probably even more significant for the Hayllars because of the particular challenges facing women artists in the nineteenth century.

A number of people have expressed astonishment to me that artists as talented as Edith and Mary felt unable to continue after marriage, and that their sisters' careers were also cut short. To understand why this might be, we need to know something of the evolving position of women artists during the nineteenth century and then see how the Hayllar daughters fit into this picture. Much excellent work has been done on this subject in recent years and we can only touch on it briefly here.[6]

In the early nineteenth century the idea prevailed that drawing and painting (especially in watercolour) was a necessary 'accomplishment' for ladies of leisure. The problem with this as a starting point for the future progress of women artists was that it led to very restrictive ideas about the sort of medium that was appropriate for them to use and the sort of subject matter that was appropriate for them to handle. It also meant that exhibiting work and seeking to sell it were considered unacceptable for women. The aims of 'accomplishments' were to make ladies more ladylike. Consequently, to engage seriously in the arts would call into question their femininity. The male establishment tended to encourage this reluctance and build on it by calling into question any feminine potential for serious painting, both in terms of physique and intellect.

The fact that lower-class women in certain parts of the country did earn their living in art-related trades, such as painting on ceramics, was dismissed as a basis for further progress, on the grounds that it did not involve the required degree of intellectual rigour.

For the art establishment to sustain this position, the fiction had to be maintained that no women artists had ever existed. Pamela Garrish Nunn tells us that

> *"Ruskin wrote in the late 1850s to a female acquaintance who aspired to become a painter, 'you must resolve to become a paintress, the feminine termination does not exist, there never having been such a being as a lady who could paint. Try to be the first…'"* [7]

In saying this, he was of course conveniently forgetting Angelika Kauffmann, Elisabeth Vigée-Lebrun, Mary Moser and very many others.

This immense social pressure against women artists took form in a number of ways other than a negative response from the critics. If women artists were by definition incapable of producing serious work, then there was no point in exhibiting it. Many found it difficult to overcome this and the Society of Female Artists was founded in 1857 to ease the situation. Similarly, there would be no point in finding places for women in educational establishments such as the Royal Academy Schools, and we considered this in Chapter 7 [see page 44].

In the mid-nineteenth century, a number of very able and determined women artists laboured to overcome these obstacles. They managed to create and exhibit work of undoubted quality, involving subject-matter which would have been considered 'male' and so the myth was gradually eroded.

Typical of them was Elizabeth Thompson (later Lady Butler) (1846-1933) whose *'Calling the Roll after an Engagement in the Crimea'* (1874) now in the Royal Collection, received much favourable comment. Ruskin's response in *Academy Notes* in 1875 was

> *"I never approached a picture with more iniquitous prejudice against it than I did Miss Thompson's: partly because I have always said no woman could paint and secondly, because I thought what the public made such a fuss about must be good for nothing."*[8]

Henrietta Ward (1832-1924)[9] also made a great contribution to the advancement of women artists, being one of the most celebrated painters of her day. She had the energy, vision and determination to combine a long career as a successful exhibiting painter with teaching, marriage and motherhood. After her husband's death in 1879 she opened a 'school for the art education of young ladies' in order to support her eight children, some of whom were still dependent on her. Another painter of the period was Joanna Mary Boyce (1831-1861)[10] whose contribution might well have been as significant as that of Henrietta Ward if it had not been for her early death.

Many women who were successful in the art world had fathers, brothers or sympathetic husbands who had made their way as painters before them. Henrietta Ward's grandfather was the well-known painter James Ward; her parents, George and Mary, were both painters and she married Michael Ward, an established artist sixteen years her senior. Similarly, Joanna Boyce was George Price Boyce's sister. This clearly had the advantage that the home environment was sympathetic to art and contacts in the art world could help to overcome the problems of securing an artistic education and then exhibiting and selling the results. The disadvantages included all the burdens of dynasties mentioned above. Women had the added difficulty that the male artists in their families were always better-known and tended to have a higher profile.

Three other painters whose careers, each in their different ways, illustrate the frustrations as well as the achievements of women artists of the period are Emma Brownlow (1832-1905), Rosa Brett (1829-1882) and Louisa Stuart, Lady Waterford (1818-1891).[11]

Emma Brownlow was an example of a woman from a middle-class background but with no artistic tradition in the family who still managed to succeed. Her aim was to earn a living as a painter, which she did until the 1870s after which she seems to have given up exhibiting. Rosa Brett made her own career and talents totally subservient to those of her brother, John Brett, who became moderately successful. Lady Waterford was an example of an aristocrat whose vision and determination lifted her work far beyond the subject-matter and technique that might have been expected of her.

By the early 1880s Ruskin's *Art of England* lectures showed that the combined effort of all these painters was clearly beginning to have an effect, even on him!

> *"For a long time I used to say in all my elementary books that, except in a graceful and minor way, women could not paint or draw. I am beginning lately, to bow myself to the much more delightful conviction that nobody else can."* [12]

By the time the Hayllar women were ready to start their exhibiting careers, some progress had been made, but there were still formidable obstacles to overcome. Firstly, they very clearly fall into the category of women artists emerging from families with a male artistic tradition. James had found it difficult to persuade his father to allow him to follow a career in art: if his daughters had been in the same position they would have found it even more difficult.

Having shown artistic talent, the next step for the Hayllars was to solve the problem of an artistic education. As we have seen, James resolved this by undertaking the work himself. By the time his daughters were ready, he could have sent them to the Slade or to the Academy Schools, but they would still have been very much in the vanguard. It was typical of the time that he chose to keep them within the domestic circle were he could exercise control. To be fair, he was obviously an inspired and thorough teacher and the education he provided clearly equipped them well for their careers as painters. On the other hand, they were denied the wider experience and social contacts that an art school education would have afforded. I think it also led them to equate painting with their childhood home and when they eventually left this home behind, painting was left behind with it.

The sort of subject matter that the Hayllar women were well-known for was not threatening to the male establishment, being very much within the domestic and family scene. On the other hand, it is very much in tune with the work of the other Wallingford artists, most of whom were men. George Leslie clearly portrayed women through the appreciative eyes of a man, but the context is very much a domestic one. The same is true of James Hayllar's own work and that of Peter Leslie while he was still in Wallingford. However, if the men in the group saw this domestic world through male eyes, the Hayllar women arguably brought a female insight to it. Edith's *'Feeding the Swans'* has been seen as an allegory for the position of women in society.[13] This message could have been seen as a threat to the male establishment, if they had been aware of it.

The Hayllar daughters had certainly moved well beyond the concept of ladies of leisure who painted a little in their spare time. Both the census returns and the tone of the critic's reception of their work in the press show that they thought of themselves as serious professional painters. All the press coverage of their work which I have found takes their work seriously. There is sometimes a certain sense of condescension, but this could be as much to do with their age as with their sex. The coverage given to Peter Leslie has a similar tone. There was, however, a fascination with the circumstances of their artistic education and the home life in which it took place.

While the Hayllar daughters were professional women, Mary Leslie was still very much cast in the mould of the 'lady of leisure'. As far as I am aware, her work was never exhibited or published, although it did come to the notice of eminent people in the art world who were friends of the family. She was of the previous generation, but this difference could also reflect the particular circumstances of her disability.

The Hayllar women do not appear to have had any difficulty exhibiting their work at the Royal Academy or at any of the other well-known venues which they used. This is a tribute, not only to the quality of their own painting, but also to the hard work of the women artists of the previous generation. Interestingly, the Hayllars do not appear to have exhibited with the Society of Female Artists, which in their time was renamed the Society of Lady Artists.

Although the Hayllars' work was seen regularly at Academy exhibitions, membership was denied them. This was a battle which would not be won for several more decades. There was actually nothing in the rules to prevent membership of women and Angelika Kauffmann and Mary Moser were among the founding members in the eighteenth century. But the nineteenth century set its face firmly against this continuing and George Leslie, writing in 1914, still viewed the prospect with undisguised horror. His objection seemed to be that he relished the exuberant behaviour of men at Academy dinners, and all this would, of course, have to stop if ladies were present. I suspect that the real reasons were too deeply rooted in prejudice to be put into print. In 1879, Elizabeth Thompson was nearly elected ARA, being defeated by two votes only. George Leslie gives a revealing account of this in his *Inner Life of the Royal Academy*, but comments that "luckily the danger passed away"! To be fair, he was referring to some clauses restricting the rights of potential women members which were hurriedly passed in response to Elizabeth Thompson's candidature. He felt that these clauses would have been damaging if they had ever been used. George had died by the time Annie Swynnerton was elected ARA in 1922 and it was not until 1936 that Dame Laura Knight became the first woman RA since the founding members.

By then the Hayllar women had long given up painting. Why? One can only guess, but I think there were several reasons. To them, painting was a serious profession which you undertook full-time or not at all. For Mary and Edith, marriage and motherhood were also full-time occupations. Their husbands would undoubtedly have agreed with them and might well have felt aggrieved if they had continued. The fact that Henry Wells did not recognise his sister-in-law's profession on the census return for 1901 may indicate a negative attitude to women artists. While important, this is clearly not the only reason. For Kate, who never married, nursing was the full-time profession which replaced painting. Ironically, if they had been ladies of leisure who painted in their spare time they might have continued longer. Another possible reason was that they needed the reassurance of buyers, and the art market had moved on. But I think the main reason was that, as I have intimated, they associated painting with the childhood home which they had left behind. For Mary this happened when she married in 1885. For Edith and Kate, it happened when their father retired and moved away, and this roughly coincided with Edith's marriage and the start of Kate's nursing career. But Jessica never did leave home, as she moved with her father to Bournemouth, and so her painting continued much longer. She finally stopped exhibiting five years before her father's death, but did not resume again afterwards.

In spite of the progress that had been achieved by contemporary women artists, the true contribution of women from earlier periods remained unrecognised. In 1971, the art historian Linda Nochlin posed the question in an extended essay *Why Have there been no Women Artists?* In answering it, she found that there had been, but their work had been unrecognised and in some cases wrongly attributed. Over the next ten years she traced a lot of this work and put together an exhibition designed to correct the story. The catalogue of the exhibition, *Women Artists 1550-1950*, has become a vital source book on the subject.[14] Our Wallingford artists have played their part in this important story as one of the paintings in the exhibition was Edith Hayllar's *'A Summer Shower'* [see page 52].

Chapter 15

QUEEN VICTORIA'S PORTRAIT

All our Wallingford artists lived on into the twentieth century but in their painting they remained quintessentially Victorian. It seems appropriate then to conclude this study of their work by looking at a remarkable joint project which James Hayllar and George Leslie undertook for the benefit of the town.

On 18th February 1887, *The Wallingford Times* reported that on the previous Thursday the Jubilee Committee had resumed its consideration of ways of commemorating the Queen's Golden Jubilee. Many ideas were considered, including the renovation of the Town Hall as we have already seen.

> *"Mr. Hayllar said in the few remarks he made in the previous meeting he incidentally mentioned that a portrait of Her Majesty might be hung in the hall. It did not meet with any response; but he now wished to say that if the Corporation would consent to take the custody of it, Mr Leslie and himself would be happy to present the town with a portrait of Her Majesty, and he did not know that they could have anything better to point to than a portrait of the Queen – (applause).*
>
> *"Alderman Hawkins expressed his pleasure… and hoped the Town Council would… memorialise the Queen, so as to get some sittings of Her Majesty for Mr Leslie and Mr Hayllar. There were very few towns that could show two artists of European reputation as they could…*
>
> *"Mr Leslie said it was a delicate matter about approaching Her Majesty, and it was not really necessary, now that there were such admirable photographs of the Queen. They proposed that the frame should be a very nice one with the arms of Wallingford upon it and a suitable inscription.*
>
> *"The Mayor… was sure that not only the committee but the whole town would be highly gratified at the very handsome offer of Mr Leslie and Mr Hayllar – (applause). He proposed that they accept it with thanks."*

In the months that followed, work obviously went ahead at some speed on the portrait and on the refurbishment of the Town Hall. Both were completed by 4th November when *The Wallingford Times* reported that

> *"Yesterday (Thursday) was appropriately called a red letter day in Wallingford… as a Grand Corporation Ball was held to open the refurbished*

Town Hall and to unveil the portrait. The ceremony was performed by Mrs Wroughton the wife of the MP."

The Mayor opened the proceedings and

"Mrs Wroughton, who was much applauded, then said : 'I have great pleasure in declaring the Town Hall open'. The Union Jack covering the picture was then removed. The portrait of the Queen… is a very fine one. In the opinion of those who have often seen the Queen, it is a most striking likeness of Her Majesty. It is in a very handsome frame and is surmounted by the Royal coat of arms…

"Mr Alderman Hawkins… proposed 'that this meeting of the inhabitants of Wallingford and its neighbourhood tenders its hearty thanks to Mr Hayllar and Mr Leslie for the noble picture of our good Queen, which they have presented to the town.' – (applause). Mr J Kirby Hedges seconded the motion… Mr Hayllar said 'I am obliged for the kind and flattering remarks you have made. I can only say it has given me great pleasure in doing it, and you are most thoroughly welcome to all I have done.' – (cheers).

"Mr Leslie, in acknowledging the vote of thanks, said the originator of the idea of presenting this picture to the town was Mr Hayllar; and to him was due the greatest share of credit, not only for having originated the idea, but for having painted the best part of the picture. He (Mr Leslie) found Mr Hayllar's work so admirable that he was afraid of spoiling it, and therefore, he had done very little, the lion's share being done by Mr Hayllar. He was glad they had not encumbered themselves with a statue of the Queen in the market-place. Statues were always troublesome, and they got dirty and smoky; but a picture came home more to the hearts of the people. A picture could hang inside and look more comfortable. Well, they had their picture of the Queen and long might she hang there' – (cheers)."

She is still there in the Town Hall, not quite in the same position but easily seen [see Fig 15.1]. It is not unique but quite rare for a painting to be created by two people and she is a fitting complement to the other work by our artists in the Town Hall.

Fig 15.1: Portrait of Her Majesty Queen Victoria by James Hayllar and George Leslie (1887). Oil

Taken as a whole, the body of their work provides us with a portrait of an age. They show us those aspects of life that interested Victorian middle-class society – aspects not always valued or approved of by subsequent generations. Consequently their work was all but forgotten. Fortunately, as we have seen, a clearer assessment of Victorian painting has now taken place.

It was in this same Hall 116 years later that I gave my first talk about these artists, from which this study has evolved. At the end I said that

> *"... they had recorded their world with great sensitivity and with consummate skill. They had done this here in Wallingford and once again it was time for Wallingford to be proud of them."*

I hope that this book will awaken an even wider enthusiasm for their work and their vision.

Fig 15.2: Wallingford Town Hall c1907, looking towards the dais where the Mayor sat. Either side of Queen Victoria are James Hayllar's 'From Grim's Dyke' and George Leslie's 'Wallingford Bridge'– including the Hayllar portraits below, that is a total of eleven paintings by our artists!

Footnotes & References

"see (1) above" refers to a previous footnote within the same chapter

Chapter 2

1 Nickola Smith, *The Leslies and the Lindfield Connection,* Nickola Smith, Lindfield 2003

2 Christopher Wood, *Dictionary of Victorian Painters,* Antique Collectors Club Ltd, 1995

3 RA library/archive, Catalogues of Summer Exhibitions, bound volumes.

4 *The Leslies and the Lindfield Connection,* see (1) above

5 'genre': paintings whose subjects are scenes of every-day life

6 Christopher Wood, *The Artistic Family Hayllar part 1,* article in *Connoisseur*, April 1974

7 George Leslie, *The Inner Life of the Royal Academy,* John Murray, London, 1914, Chaps 2 & 3

Chapter 3

1 Verbal: Bob Woodings. Constable's letter to CR Leslie of 6th July 1835 reads "Dear Leslie, I hope the bearer of this note will bring us good accounts of Mrs Leslie and that you are relieved of all your anxiety." RB Beckett, *John Constables's Correspondence with CR Leslie RA,* Suffolk Records Society Vol VII, 1965

2 George Leslie, *The Inner Life of the Royal Academy,* John Murray, London, 1914, pages 140-143

3 Nickola Smith, *The Leslies and the Lindfield Connection,* Nickola Smith, Lindfield 2003

4 RA Library/archive, Catalogues of Summer Exhibitions

5 RA library/archive, Election book commencing 1866

6 Catalogue, *The Forbes Collection of Victorian Pictures and Works of Art, Vol 3,* Christie's, London, 2003, page 163

7 George Leslie, *Letters to Marco,* Macmillan and Co, London 1893, page 8

8 George Leslie, *Riverside Letters,* Macmillan and Co, London 1896, page 26

9 Vivien Knight, *Victorian Pictures,* Guildhall Art Gallery, Guildhall Art Gallery Publications, London, 1999

10 *The Leslies and the Lindfield Connection,* see (3) above) and Tate Archive 9613.5.2

11 Verbal: Janet Anderson

12 George Leslie, *Our River,* 2nd Edition, Bradbury Agnew and Co, London, 1888

13 *The Leslies and the Lindfield Connection*, see (3) above, page 25

14 All extracts from *The Berks and Oxon Advertiser* and *The Wallingford Times* can be found at the Centre for Oxfordshire Studies

Chapter 4

1 Nickola Smith, *The Leslies and the Lindfield Connection,* Nickola Smith, Lindfield 2003, page 13

2 Verbal: Connie Wilder

3 Tate Archive 9613.4

Chapter 5

1 *The Berks & Oxon Advertiser,* 14th June 1895

2 Nickola Smith, *The Leslies and the Lindfield Connection,* Nickola Smith, Lindfield 2003, page 20

3 RA library/archive, Catalogues of Summer Exhibitions.

4 *The Leslies and the Lindfield Connection,* see (1) above, page 20

5 *The Leslies and the Lindfield Connection,* see (1) above, page 30

6 *The Leslies and the Lindfield Connection,* see (1) above, page 43

Chapter 6

1 Mervyn Cutten and Brian Stewart, *Chichester Artists, 1530-1900,* Bladon Press, Canterbury, 1987, pages 22-23

2 Christopher Wood, *The Artistic Family Hayllar part 1,* article in *Connoisseur,* April 1974

3 Verbal: Lois Jenkins.

4 RA library/archive, Catalogues of Summer Exhibitions.

5 *The Artistic Family Hayllar, part 1,* see (2) above

6 RA library/archive, Election Book commencing 1866

7 RBA archive (held at V&A Museum archives, Blythe House, 23 Blythe Road London W14 0QF) Register of Members 1824-1900, AAD/1997/8/49

8 RBA archive, Council Minutes 1886-1893, AAD/1997/8/10

9 Christopher Wood, *Paradise Lost,* Trafalgar Square Publishing, North Pumfret, Vermont, 1989, page 139

10 *The Artistic Family Hayllar, part 1,* see (2) above

11 *The Artistic Family Hayllar, part 1,* see (2) above

12 David Beasley and Judy & Stuart Dewey, *Window on Wallingford 1837-1914,* Pie Powder Press, Cholsey, 1989, numerous references to Edward Wells

13 *The Berks and Oxon Advertiser,* 25th Feb 1921

14 *The Artistic Family Hayllar, part 1,* see (2) above

Chapter 7

1 *Ladies Pictorial,* Dec 1889 as reported in *The Berks and Oxon Advertiser,* Jan 31, 1890

2 Verbal: Lois Jenkins

3 Anthony Lester in a video made for Scope at Castle Priory, now in the possession of Ray Johnson

4 RA library/archive, Catalogues of Summer Exhibitions

5 Verbal: Neil Mackay

6 George Leslie, *The Inner Life of the Royal Academy,* John Murray, London, 1914, pages 42-43

7 Abigail Large, *The Hayllar Sisters,* BA dissertation, unpublished, University of Aberystwyth, 1996

8 David Beasley and Judy & Stuart Dewey, *Window on Wallingford 1837-1914,* Pie Powder Press, Cholsey, 1989

9 Verbal: Daphne Brookes

Chapter 8

1 Abigail Large, *The Hayllar Sisters,* BA dissertation, unpublished, University of Aberystwyth, 1996

2 Catalogue, *The Forbes Collection of Victorian Pictures and Works of Art,* Christie's, London 2003, Vol 2 page 144

3 *The Hayllar Sisters,* see (1) above

4 Although a sketch book study of Lake Lucerne dates from 1910, see Chapter 14

5 Christopher Wood, *The Artistic Family Hayllar, part 2,* article in *Connoisseur,* May 1974

Chapter 9

1 RA library/archive, Catalogues of Summer Exhibitions

2 Abigail Large, *The Hayllar Sisters,* BA dissertation, unpublished, University of Aberystwyth, 1996

3 RA library /archive, Catalogues of Summer Exhibitions

4 Verbal: Ada Lay

5 Verbal: Lois Jenkins

Chapter 10

1 Christopher Wood, *The Artistic Family Hayllar, part 2,* article in *Connoisseur,* May 1974

2 Abigail Large, *The Hayllar Sisters,* BA dissertation, unpublished, University of Aberystwyth, 1996

3 Catalogue, *The Forbes Collection of Victorian Pictures and Works of Art,* Christie's, London 2003, Vol 2 page 147 and Robyn Asleson et al, *Pre-Raphaelite and Other Masters in the Andrew Lloyd Webber Collection,* RA, London, 2003

4 Verbal: Arthur & Nancy Carver

Chapter 11

1 All the background information on the Rowbotham family in this chapter is drawn from Anthony Lester's article *The Rowbotham Family, Two Centuries of Artistic Talent,* Antique Collecting, Vol 18 No 5 (Oct 1983) pages 35-39 (the Journal of the Antique Collectors' Club telephone (01394) 389950)

2 Berkshire Record Office *D/EH E26*

Chapter 12

1 Figures for RA from Catalogues of Summer Exhibitions held in RA library/archive. Those for RBA from catalogues in RBA archive, AAD/1997/8. Figures for Claude Rowbotham from Anthony Lester, *The Rowbotham Family, Two Centuries of Artistic Talent,* Antique Collecting, Vol 18 No 5 (Oct 1983). All others from Christopher Wood, *Dictionary of Victorian Painters,* Antique Collectors Club Ltd, 1995

2 Tate Archive, George Leslie's day book, 9613.5.2

3 George Leslie, *The Inner Life of the Royal Academy,* John Murray, London, 1914, pages 121 and 123

4 RBA archive, AAD/1997/8

5 Photocopy kindly provided for me by Ray Johnson

6 RBA archive AAD/1997/8

7 Information extracted for me by the archivist of the Royal Institute of Painters in Watercolour

8 From Christie's website, 2003

9 RA Archive

10 RA Archive

11 Quoted in George Leslie's obituary, *The Berks and Oxon Advertiser,* 25th February 1921

12 Tate Archive, George Leslie's day book 9613.5.2

13 Robyn Asleson et al, *Pre-Raphaelite and Other Masters in the Lloyd Webber Collection,* RA, London, 2003, p98

14 Nickola Smith, *The Leslies and the Lindfield Connection,* Nickola Smith, Lindfield 2003, page 13

15 Tate Archive, Peter Leslie's notebook, 9613.6.2

Chapter 13

1 Information from *The Reading Chronicle,* June 29th 1979, article by Leslie North. Berkshire Archives

2 David Beasley and Judy & Stuart Dewey, *Window on Wallingford 1837-1914,* Pie Powder Press, Cholsey, 1989

Chapter 14

1 Tate Archive, George Leslie's day book

2 Obituary of James Hayllar, *The Berks and Oxon Advertiser,* 12th March 1920

3 Verbal: Ada Lay

4 Edward Morris, *Victorian and Edwardian Paintings in the Lady Leaver Art Gallery,* London, HMSO, 1994

5 Tate Archive, George Leslie's day book

6 Pamela Gerrish Nunn, *Victorian Women Artists,* The Women's Press, London, 1987; Deborah Cherry, *Painting Women: Victorian Women Artists,* Routledge, 1993; Ann Sutherland Harris and Linda Nochlin, *Women Artists, 1550-1950,* Los Angeles County Museum of Art, Alfred A Knopf, New York, 1981

7 *Victorian Women Artists,* see (6), page 16

8 *Victorian Women Artists,* see (6), page 132

9 *Victorian Women Artists,* see (6), page 146

10 *Victorian Women Artists,* see (6), page 16

11 *Victorian Women Artists,* see (6), pages 158, 187 and 174 respectively

12 Abigail Large, *The Hayllar Sisters,* BA dissertation, unpublished, University of Aberystwyth, 1996

13 George Leslie, *The Inner Life of the Royal Academy,* John Murray, London, 1914, pages 222-223

14 *Women Artists, 1550-1950,* see (6), pages 258-259

FAMILY TREES

KEY

(??)	= Date or Name unknown
Name in CAPITALS	= Artist
NAME IN GREY BOX	= Artist featured in this book

The Leslie Dynasty

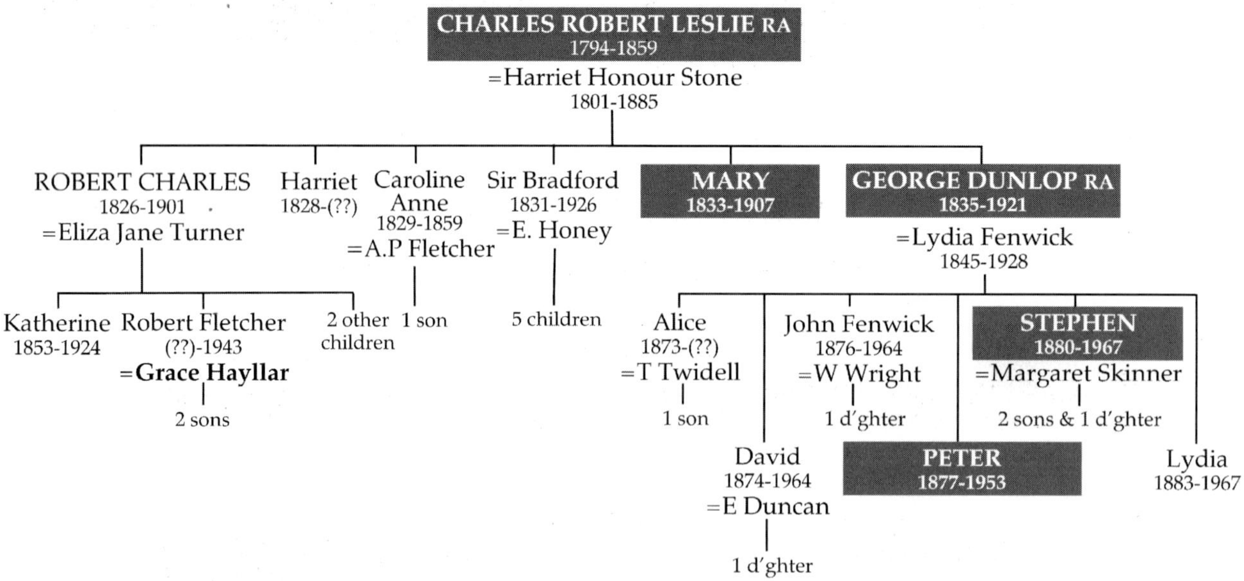

The Hayllar Dynasty

JAMES HAYLLAR RBA
1828-1920
=Ellen Phoebe Cavell
1827-1901

- Ernest Theodore
  1856-(??)
- Reginald James
  1858-(??)
- **JESSICA ELLEN**
  1858-1940
- **EDITH PARVIN**
  1860-1948
  =Rev Edward Bruce Mackay
  - 4 children
- Eugene Grace
  1861-(??)
  =**Robert Fletcher Leslie**
  - 2 children
- **ALEXANDRA MARY**
  1863-1950
  = Henry Wells
  - 6 children
- **BEATRICE KATE**
  1864-1956
- Thomas Leopold
  1866-1902
- Algernon Victor
  1868-(??)

The Rowbotham Dynasty

THOMAS LEESON SCARSE ROWBOTHAM
1783-1853

- THOMAS CHARLES LEESON
  1823-1875
  =Ellen Amelia (??)
  - CHARLES EDMOND
    1856-1921
    - LEOPOLD CHARLES LEESON
      1889-1977
      (trained as painter but became bank manager)
  - 6 other children
  - **CLAUDE HAMILTON**
    1864-1949
    =Lizzie (??)
    1859-(??)
    - Howard
      1893-(??)
    - Louie
      1894-(??)
    - Bronwin
      1899-(??)
- MISS E (probably EMMA
  1840-(??)
- Other children

Acknowledgements

Thanks are due first to The Wallingford Historical and Archaeological Society for inviting me to give the talk that led to this book and encouraging me to transform the one into the other.

I have received valuable help from a number of art historians and thanks are particularly due to Nickola Smith for generously sharing her research into the Leslies at Lindfield, Ann Stieglitz for her enthusiasm and specific information on the position of women artists, Anthony Lester for permission to quote his research on the Rowbotham family, Abigail Large for permission to use her research on the Hayllar sisters, Marygai Hayllar for an Australian perspective, Simon Jones for background information, and Christopher Wood for putting me in touch with Neil Mackay.

Neil was the first descendant of these artists I met. He helped me with the original talk and knew that the book was in preparation. I was very sad that he did not live to see it published. Other family members have also been unstinting in their support, including Fanny Mackay, Bruce Mackay, Anne Hammond, Lois Jenkins and Daphne Brookes. Ronan Leslie and his sister Avril Bacon and her family gave David Beasley and me a great time when we visited them in Norfolk. Without them the book would be much the poorer.

Other people in Wallingford have also been very helpful with information and advice, including Janet Anderson, Mary Bitmead and her daughter Elizabeth Parker, Steve Capel-Davies, Arthur and Nancy Carver, Wendy Cook, Anna Crowe, Sue Hendrie, Jo Heydon, Ray Johnson, Ada Lay, Ray and Carole Neag, Andrew Rogers, Connie Wilder, David Wilder, Richard Wilder and Bob Woodings.

The book would not have happened without David Beasley who not only provided many of the photographs but also has an encyclopaedic knowledge of *The Berks and Oxon Advertiser* and *The Wallingford Times*. We shared many good laughs in the last three years!

Many thanks are also due to my wife Anne for reading the text and putting up with my 'Hayllar and Leslie obsession'. Finally, thanks to my old friends Judy and Stuart Dewey of Pie Powder Press for taking on the publishing.

Anthony Wilder, Wallingford, 2006

Picture Credits

I am very grateful to the following organisations and individuals for permission to reproduce their paintings and photographs. Illustrations are listed by Figure No:

Copyright Christie's Images Ltd 2006 . . . 6.3, 7.2, 7.5, 9.1
Guildhall Art Gallery, Corporation of London . . . 3.8, 10.2
Lindfield Parish Council . . . 5.4
Lord Lloyd Webber . . . 8.2, 10.5
Manchester City Galleries . . . 3.7
National Museums, Liverpool (Walker Art Gallery) . . . 3.5
National Museums, Liverpool (Lady Lever Art Gallery) . . . 6.5, 14.1
Courtesy of NR Omell Gallery . . . 3.6
Private Collection, Photo courtesy Christopher Wood . . . 6.4
Royal Academy of Arts, London . . . 3.3
Sotheby's . . . 9.6
St Leonard's Church, Wallingford (photo by Judy Dewey) . . . 13.4
Photo Tate Archive . . . 4.1, 4.2, 4.3, 4.4, 4.5
Tate, London, 2005 . . . 2.1, 2.2, 3.4, 3.12
Wallingford Town Council (photos by David Beasley/Stuart Dewey) . . . 3.1, 3.11, 6.1, 6.8, 6.9, 7.3, 7.7, 15.1
Wallingford Museum . . . 13.1, 13.3

All the other paintings are in private collections and I am very grateful to the owners (all of whom wish to remain anonymous) for generously allowing me to use them, with original photography by David Beasley, digitally processed by Stuart Dewey.

Index of Names and Places

Page numbers in **bold** refer to illustrations

Index of Picture Titles

Page numbers in **bold** refer to illustrations

Fig 15.3: Windmill in the Landscape by James Hayllar (1890). Oil